the
BARRENS

the
BARRENS

A NOVEL OF LOVE AND DEATH
IN THE CANADIAN ARCTIC

KURT JOHNSON
AND ELLIE JOHNSON

ARCADE PUBLISHING • NEW YORK

First Edition

This is a work of fiction. Names, places, characters, and incidents are either the products of the author's imagination or are used fictitiously.

Arcade Publishing books may be purchased in bulk at special discounts for sales promotion, corporate gifts, fund-raising, or educational purposes. Special editions can also be created to specifications. For details, contact the Special Sales Department, Arcade Publishing, 307 West 36th Street, 11th Floor, New York, NY 10018 or arcade@skyhorsepublishing.com.

Arcade Publishing® is a registered trademark of Skyhorse Publishing, Inc.®, a Delaware corporation.

Visit our website at www.arcadepub.com.
Visit the authors at www.kurtjohnsonbooks.com.

"Galileo" words and music by Emily Saliers. Copyright © 1992 GODHAP MUSIC. All Rights controlled and administered by SONGS OF UNIVERSAL, INC. All Rights Reserved. Used by Permission. *Reprinted by permission of Hal Leonard LLC*

10 9 8 7 6 5 4 3 2

Library of Congress Cataloging-in-Publication Data is available on file.
Library of Congress Control Number: 2021949518

Cover design by Erin Seaward-Hiatt
Cover images © Drlogan/Getty Images (topographical lines); © Westend61/Getty Images (canoers); © Pobytov/Getty Images (painting)
Author photo courtesy of Stephanie Hansen

ISBN: 978-1-950994-48-9
Ebook ISBN: 978-1-950994-62-5

Printed in the United States of America

For Stephanie—Wife and Mother

PART ONE

THE STORYIST

1

A precarious chest-high pile of stacked and balanced rocks, a cairn, marked the Thelon Canyon portage. As I pulled the canoe up onto the shore, I saw a white piece of paper protruding from between two cairn rocks like a fortune from a broken cookie. I lifted a stone and pinched it out. The paper was thin, yellowed, and brittle with a message written in faded pencil. It said, "This 1,200-rod portage sucks ass." It was signed, "Schuyler, Camp Kawishiwi, 7/11/18." Two summers earlier. I showed it to Holly and she smiled. She knew Schuyler—they'd been together on Camp Kawishiwi canoe trips back in high school, four years ago. She said that the notes were a backcountry ritual, a legacy of the fur trade. The handwritten scraps were how the lone trappers communicated—one leaving a message for the other, often attesting to their last known whereabouts.

Holly said it would take us all day to do the 1,200-rod, four-mile portage with our four packs of gear. She pulled at the bill of my cap, smiled, and kissed me—a peck on the lips. She said, "It's your turn to carry the canoe." We were twelve days in and Holly was keeping score.

The canoe could wait. On the first crossing we both carried our lighter personal packs with our clothes, tents, sleeping bags, and miscellaneous stuff. The packs, known as P-packs, were strapped over our life vests. I lifted my paddle and followed Holly up a steep switchback trail.

The portage took us inland, away from the river, to the highest point of a bluff that stretched in every direction atop what seemed to be miles of sandstone shelf. Holly led and she followed the cairns, spaced just close enough so that from one you could see the other. I heard the whitewater before seeing it, water crashing through rocks. A mist rose through a slit in the shelf. We walked over and looked down into the deep gorge of the canyon. Below was a six-foot waterfall and a set of turbulent rapids that would've crushed and swamped our canoe had we not chosen to portage.

Holly pulled out her iPhone to take a photo. She had me stand with my back to the edge of the bluff, the canoe paddle held across my waist like a hunting rifle. She told me to push my hair away from my face, lift my chin, and smile. I tucked both curtains of hair back over each ear, then looked toward the iPhone. She said, "Come on, Lee, smile." I smiled as best I could, closed lips over teeth that had never been straightened. She took the photo. I stepped back and Holly moved to the edge herself. She held the phone at arm's length high above her head to take a selfie with the water and rapids in the distance. Then Holly moved one foot back to pose, the heel just touching the edge. I saw what she was doing was dangerous and for a split second I wanted to shout something—*be careful* or *get away from the ledge*—but I was too late, too slow. I could've said something, but I didn't.

The sandstone gave way and her back foot slipped. The phone dropped to the ground, and her body tipped and pitched backward. I shouted, "Holly," and ran toward her, but she was too far away and I couldn't stop her from falling. I saw her face for a split second—eyes and mouth wide open, no sound, no scream. Surprise, that's all it was. Just surprise before plummeting into the abyss. And then she was gone beyond the slit in the stone, disappearing into the mist. I ran to the edge, knelt, and looked down. Hoping.

The canyon walls were sheer, with a three-story drop to the whitewater below. I saw the red of her life vest and the olive green of the P-pack an arm's length away. She descended through the rapids, and I watched her head bob up for a breath and her hands reach for anything that might provide an anchor in the current. I dropped my pack and ran along the edge of the canyon and followed her through the maze of rocks. Her pack drifted faster and farther away. I kept my eyes on Holly. I thought that if I lost eye contact for one second, I'd lose her. I needed to be close to the edge to see her and help her, and I fought an impulse to lunge over the edge and save her, but I saw only jagged rocks within the cascading whitewater, no pooling where I could safely land. I'd end up just as fucked. And there was still hope, she was still bobbing and gasping for air. Then Holly spilled over a three-foot ledge and into the backflow of water. Her body was caught in the undertow and I saw her pushed in and under the drop, then out, then back in, tumbling over and over, stuck in that hole's endless cycle. The P-pack tumbled with her, then broke open, scattering clothes.

I stepped back from the edge, losing eye contact with Holly tumbling in the hole. I needed to be there when her body was spit out and pushed farther down the canyon. I ran and followed the cairns. The gorge widened and the bluff walls became less sheer. I searched to find a way to the water's edge. I saw a ravine and scrambled down the loose rock—scree. As the ravine steepened, I turned backward on all fours, finding footing as best I could. Then I slipped and slid with the sharp edges of the scree scraping into my thighs. I fell over a ledge and for a weightless moment thought I would die, that this was how my nightmare would end. I hit the slope of the ravine, then took one headfirst tumble, then another, and my forehead hit solid rock. I tumbled again and then slid face-first down the incline until I stopped at the river-level bottom.

I saw the exit to the gorge, the water eddying back toward me. Pieces of clothing from the P-pack floated by. I waded into the eddy and saw a pair of underpants, but they were my underpants, the boxers I wore. And I realized that Holly had been carrying my P-pack and I'd had hers. The pack floated toward me, torn and nearly empty. Left tucked inside was my sleeping bag that kept the pack afloat. I still didn't see Holly. As I waited, my legs became numb in the frigid water, but my face flushed hot with perspiration. I was shaking from fear, panic. I waited and time magnified. I forced myself to breathe.

I saw the red of Holly's life vest. I saw her shoulders and wisps of hair flowing from the back of her head. She floated past the eddy, and I ran back to shore and followed as she drifted downstream and then slowly came to a stop. I waded in and staggered through the river, my thighs pumping against water, my feet finding purchase on the rocky bottom. I slipped on a rock and submerged into the cold water, then stood and kept moving until I was at Holly's side and had a hand through the armhole of her vest. I turned her over. Bloody lacerations covered the side of her face like claw marks. She wasn't breathing. My lips met hers to move air, my fingers holding her nose closed. I kept trying as I pulled her body to shallow water. I took a deep breath for both of us, a step, another breath. Her limp body sagged in the vest. I pulled her onto the shore, still delivering a breath for her, for me. Blood dripped from the cut on my forehead and onto her face, merging with her blood, swirling in the current like wisps of smoke. I thought I was losing her, that she was dying and leaving me alone on the Barrens.

I felt her body shake and convulse. She coughed water. Then took a breath.

2

Two weeks earlier we'd purchased the canoe in the remote Canadian mining town of Yellowknife, nine hundred miles north of Edmonton.

I'd only known Holly then for six months, both of us college students at Brown. We'd met at a coffee shop in College Hill where she found me doing homework. I was wearing the opposite of pretty-girl clothes—a flannel shirt, jeans, and work boots with my hair tied up in a sloppy topknot. She just sat down and said, "What are you doing?" I said that I was doing homework—my obvious, unwitty response. Then I guess her idea of a pickup tactic was to start telling me what *we* should do—"We should have coffee together, next week we should go to see this show." I dated Holly on and off for a few months before she said that we should do this canoe trip on the Thelon River way up near the Arctic Circle. She'd been there before and really wanted to go back. And I thought, *Why the fuck not*. I had few other options while college was on break for the summer—there was no going home, no home to go back to. My options were either to travel with Holly or work at some restaurant in Providence. I said okay. In retro-spect, I think I was the only friend she'd been able to coax into going back to the Thelon with her.

We bought the canoe from a guy who'd advertised it for sale on Craigslist. We called him and walked the mile or so to the texted address. His house was like most of what we'd seen in Yellowknife—a mobile home, a picture window on the hitch end overlooking a gravel road, a stainless-steel chimney, a pickup out front. This house stuck out because of a barbed wire–topped chain-link fence that surrounded the property. Inside the fence was an assortment of stuff—a snowmobile, half a snowmobile, a pile of scrap wood, two empty dog kennels, a pop-up camper, a stack of firewood as tall as me, and this red canoe that lay upside down on top of the stack, I assumed to keep the wood dry. It was the canoe we wanted. We needed it to paddle the 450 miles down the Thelon River through the Arctic Barren Lands to Baker Lake.

Holly helped him lift the canoe off the pile and rest it right side up on the dirt driveway. The guy looked to be in his forties. His uncut hair hung long from under a knit cap. His face had a short stubble that probably hadn't been shaved in a week. Two inches shorter and he could have been the younger brother of my father, Jake the Snake. Same threadbare shirt worn through at the elbows. Same steel-toed work boots that looked two sizes too big. Jake would've liked this guy who lived on the edge of nowhere.

The canoe had a story, so the guy said. I stood behind Holly; she would do the negotiating because she had the money.

He said, "That canoe is a short fifteen-foot Royalex Mad River Quest. I was working for an outfitter out of Fort Smith, and one year we hired on this old man that had moved out to the Territories from somewhere in England. His name was John something-or-other, but we called him Jack, for that writer Jack London. Jack had been canoeing the Barrens alone for a few summers and pretty much living the life of a monk. The Mad River Quest was his canoe, and I figure that over the years, it had seen every major river—the Thelon, the Hanbury, the Burntside, the Back, the Lockhart, the Coppermine, and some rivers that had no names. So, he got hired on as a wilderness guide. But Jack turned out to be kind of squirrelly. He was particular about what he'd eat and brought along a mixed bag of dried caribou, dried fruit, nuts, and what have you. He said the mix was all you needed to sustain life. He was like a dog that eats nothing but dog food. He rarely washed, and the tourists complained about his smell. And he wouldn't do the whole show-and-tell thing like bear and wolf stories, pointing out birds, edible plants, or the ways of the Inuit. So, he lasted only the one season and then went back to paddling the Arctic rivers each summer by himself, living hand to mouth.

"Well, a year later, he didn't show up at Fort Smith when the snow fell in September and winter started to set in. By the time we figured we should go looking for him, the lakes and rivers were freezing up. The Mounties did flyovers searching for any sign of a campfire, but they found nothing. It wasn't until August of the next year that on one of my guided trips I stumbled upon the canoe and what remained of Jack London. I figured he'd tried to run the Muskox Rapids on the Coppermine but got turned sideways. What we found were just picked bones and pieces of clothing washed up on shore. His canoe was found farther down, past a waterfall that would've crushed any aluminum canoe like a beer can. So, I dragged the canoe out and kept it. My kids don't have much interest in anything that doesn't have an engine, so it never gets used."

Holly stood there with one hand on her hip. She wore a straw cowboy hat with the sides rolled, not a cowboy thing really, more like a tourist hat from Mexico. I thought she looked cute—she *was* cute. She looked at the canoe and shook her head.

"That's a horrible story," she said. "So, this is a dead man's canoe? You want to sell us a canoe that a man died in?"

"You don't get it. Jack London paddled this canoe by himself a thousand or more miles each season for eight seasons. Jack might have died in the rapids, but the canoe went through those rapids and over a frickin' waterfall! She still floats and is probably good for another ten thousand miles. This canoe is tested and proven. And these Royalex hulls are the toughest ever built."

I said nothing. Jake and I once had a canoe out on the Platte River that we used for fishing and duck hunting. It was an aluminum canoe painted camo brown with a square stern where we attached a small two-horse motor. We paddled some, but that was the extent of my canoe knowledge. What I did know was that canoes were supposed to have seats, one in front and one in back, and this canoe had neither. I said nothing because Holly was right there with it.

"There are no seats," she said.

"Old-timers, especially solo canoeists, like to paddle on their knees. Jack took out the seats a long time ago. But you'll get used to it—you sit more upright, get a better stroke and a better look around. The bowman can see rocks ahead more clearly. Paddling on your knees is safer. And just to be honest, you're not going to find a better canoe in all of Yellowknife, at least not a Royalex, not one for sale, and not for four hundred dollars."

And that was a fact. We'd been camping just outside of town for the past three days. We'd asked around, checked online, and looked at a catalog of new canoes that cost over two thousand dollars, but those had to be shipped from Edmonton, a week away, with additional freight costs. And we weren't traveling back to college with the canoe after the summer was over. A used throwaway canoe would work just fine.

Also, I was sick of Yellowknife and ready to move on. The campground was littered with broken beer bottles and empty pints of Fireball whiskey, the place used by townie boys at night to have bonfires and get wasted. We seemed to be the only two women around, and some were starting to get bold and holler at us in our tent to come out and party. It was getting uncomfortable, and I was anxious just thinking about what I'd do if one touched the zipper on our tent—yell, scream, or worse. I was ready to get out of that dump, and I hoped Holly was thinking the same thing.

She inspected the canoe, ran her hand down the length of the hull, and then checked each thwart. Finally, she said, "Fine, if you throw in two paddles."

The next day, when we loaded the canoe with the four packs and knelt in the bow and stern, the canoe sank deep into the water. Evidently our fifteen-foot canoe was short, seventeen being the standard. What was called the freeboard—the distance between the waterline and the top edge of the canoe—was about four inches. It looked like a slight shift of weight or waves on a windy lake could easily swamp the thing.

3

The summer Arctic sun never completely set, never gave us the extended darkness of night that my body instinctively craved for sleep, and I slept poorly. I was up for good when the sun rose just beneath the horizon and filled the tent with a red glow magnified by the red of the nylon walls. I crawled out of my sleeping bag, dressed, and walked to the water's edge with the one fat book I'd brought along for the trip. The sky in the northeast was a watercolor of reds and oranges that stretched up from the tops of stunted black spruce and reflected pastel purple off the thin stratus clouds overhead. Beautiful. Then an edge of the sun rose and the pale rays slowly pushed away the colors of dawn. For the next few hours before Holly woke, I lay on the shore with my head in the crook of my elbow and read intermittently. One line from the book, *Arctic Dreams*, stuck with me, "Everything was held together by stories. That's all that was holding us together, stories and compassion." It was something Holly would say.

Being this far north felt like an escape into another world, like everything south existed in some alternate universe that couldn't touch me now. But I knew it wasn't so much the place as the distance traveled. We'd driven Holly's Audi three thousand miles northwest from Providence, crossing Canada above the Great Lakes—thirty hours nonstop, alternating at the wheel as each of us became drowsy. We stored the car in Winnipeg and then boarded the eight-hour flight with a stop in Edmonton, on through to Yellowknife. Holly and I were far from our homes, families, and the rarefied life of college. And later that morning we would take another plane, a *bush* plane, deep into the Barren Lands to where the Thelon River began and civilization ended. I dozed on and off, thoughts entering and leaving my mind like waves on a beach.

Holly crawled through the opening in the tent when the sun had already made its way clockwise from the north, rose past the treetops, and now floated just above the nearby superstructure of an abandoned gold mine. From what we'd heard, the Giant Mine had a long, painful life—nine strikebreakers killed in a bombing in 1992, then the mine abandoned by its owners in 2004, leaving behind 200,000 tons of deadly arsenic trioxide dust. The pollution bothered Holly, her special place spoiled. She set a pot of coffee on our camp stove and lit the burner.

Most of our supplies were packed and ready to go in four worn olive-green canvas Duluth Packs. Two were food packs weighing eighty pounds each with enough nonperishable stuff to last us the forty days. The other two were the lighter P-packs that along with our personal stuff held tents, ropes, duct tape, a fishing rod with tackle, water bottles, a first-aid kit, a Leatherman multi-tool, and six marked-up topographical maps for each stretch of the river. Most of this gear Holly had purchased in Yellowknife. Our trip on water would start with a short paddle across the Great Slave Lake to Latham Island, where the bush planes, perched on their slender floats, were docked.

Before we set off across the lake, Holly gave me a brief lesson in paddling. What I knew from being with Jake on the Platte didn't cut it. She showed me the proper way to get into the canoe, stepping only on the centerline, the keel, to keep the canoe from tipping—"You tip, you fall, you get wet, you get hypothermia, you could die," she said. There was a bow, the front, and a bow-man, or bow person. There was a C-stroke, J-stroke, box stroke, draw stroke, pry stroke, sweep stroke, and a forward stroke—I'd not known there were different strokes all with names. Before we set off, Holly had me practice each stroke while kneeling on the edge of the dock. Once in the canoe, we both wore life vests, and clipped into a mesh pocket on Holly's vest was a PLB, Personal Locator Beacon, used to call in Canadian Search and Rescue if we had an emergency. Holly paddled stern, the rear, from where the boat was steered, while I'd be learning how to paddle from the bow. We used our dense foam sleeping mats doubled over to cushion our knees for paddling without seats. Right away, Holly complained that I wasn't paddling hard enough. She said, "Stop lily-dipping." I wanted to say something back, *Fuck you,* or *Back off,* or maybe *What the hell am I doing here,* but I kept quiet and just dug in harder. The edge of my paddle blade made a small whirlpool, a vortex of water, a toilet flush. By the time we reached the bush plane docks, my thighs had begun to cramp and my knees felt numb, deadened.

Holly led me to a whitewashed one-story building with an old backlit Royal Crown Cola sign with lettering beneath that spelled out WATERDROME. When we walked through the door, the faces of ten or more, I assumed pilots, looked our way. They stared silently like cows in a pasture. We stood and let them get a good look. And I was just a little self-conscious. I could tell what they were thinking, or I thought I could tell—a couple of lesbians. I knew I looked the part. I was big and wore the same shirts as Jake always had, the same pants. We were almost the same size and shared just about everything. But I was not altogether the complete package. I had long hair, no side mullet, and I didn't have piercings in my face. I liked my look and Holly liked it, too. She called it androgynous, like she didn't care *what* I was. Holly stepped forward and broke the silence among the cluster of pilots, "Is Knute here?"

They all turned at once and looked toward a man in coveralls who was filling his coffee cup from a Bunn glass decanter. He was old, like mid-seventies, and wore a black cap with the embroidered words, *Vietnam Veteran*. What immediately made me nervous was the pair of thick glasses he wore with one lens blacked out. Despite that, the guy was clean-cut, with official-looking patches on his khaki coveralls. He said, "I'm Knute."

KNUTE TALKED ABOUT his prized plane while we helped load. The de Havilland Beaver was one of only five built in their last year of production in 1967, one of two still flying. I wanted to ask what happened to the other three but kept my mouth shut and just listened and watched. The single engine bolted to its nose had a beehive of air-cooled cylinders that circled the shaft of a three-bladed propeller. Inside, the plane could hold six passengers with ample room in the tail section for cargo. We loaded our packs and then helped Knute lash the Royalex Mad River Quest onto the struts of one float. The canoe extended halfway down the plane's fuselage and looked out of place next to the sleek lines of riveted aluminum. I vaguely understood aerodynamics, the idea of air circulating above and below the smooth surfaces of nimble wings, and the canoe seemed like a hazardous rumble strip impeding airflow. I didn't see how a canoe lashed to the outside of a plane was a good idea, how any of this was a good idea, but I trusted that Knute had done this a thousand times during his countless years of flying. Then I got a good look at him from the side, and I could see the well of an eyeball-less socket, and I wanted to ask how a one-eyed septuagenarian could get a pilot license in Canada.

Our four Duluth packs were stowed behind the seats. Holly sat up front with Knute. Both wore lime-green headphones that covered their ears, with a wanded mic they could use to talk with each other. I sat behind her with no headphones and just the loud drone of the engine grinding away in my skull. We left the dock and pushed north into the oncoming waves. Then Knute levered the throttle forward, the engine screamed, and in seconds we lifted off and passed over the island. In the distance I saw our campground get smaller and smaller, and I was thinking that every time we took off or glided down a highway entrance ramp, each mile we'd driven and flown, got me farther away, removed, so that maybe I could look back on my life as though it were the life of another girl. I wanted to let go and tell that story.

Holly and I didn't really know that much about each other. I'd never met her parents, and she'd never met Jake. She knew enough about him and where I'd grown up so that I didn't look as though I kept secrets, but I did. And Holly? She acted all cagey like she was ashamed or embarrassed about her upbringing and wealth. But that was *her* baggage, and I could've cared less. Maybe with all the time we'd have on the river without school, television, or internet—just the two of us—maybe we would both just let go.

The sky was cloudless, and I could see straight down. I saw as much water as land, water in mostly smaller lakes and ponds that from this altitude looked like the thousands of little puddles that collected in every pothole of Jake's dirt driveway after a downpour. Surrounding the lakes were eruptions of hard gray rock. The rocks were mottled green with lichens, shrubs, and spindly trees. The land in the distance looked cornfield flat with few distinguishing characteristics other than water and tundra. It did seem barren.

The plane started its descent, and I felt it in my ears. We were being dropped off on Lynx Lake, the headwaters of the Thelon, and we planned to spend the rest of July and two weeks in August paddling to where the river ended at Baker Lake.

Landing in a small plane with floats for wheels seemed impossible and frightening, as though we were likely to hit the water hard, somersault, and burst into a thousand bloody pieces. As Knute did a first pass low over Lynx Lake, Holly pushed her finger against the Plexiglas window, pointing, and I looked down to see the lake funneling toward the narrow entrance to the Thelon that snaked in the distance. The sand beneath the shallow water reflected the sunlight and turned the river a stunning vibrant green. We flew lower and I saw the whitecaps of windblown waves and the reefs of gunpowder-gray rock. I guessed Knute was looking for anything that might slash at the thin aluminum of our floats. He gunned the engine and turned in a wide circle, then came in for his final approach. The engine all but cut, leaving a near absence of sound that was both frightening and calming, like I imagined the pause between when a hanged man drops, just before the line goes taut and snaps his neck. The gruesome analogy jolted me out of the fear I was experiencing, and I found myself smiling morbidly. We glided and then touched the water with little more than a quiet splash. I was still alive.

Knute revved the engine, taxied toward a beach near the river's entrance, pushed the nose of the floats up onto the sand, then cut the engine. Holly stepped out onto the floats, and I started handing down packs to her, which she then carried to the shore. Knute unstrapped our canoe from the struts and set it in the water.

Before he left, Knute stood with us onshore. The canoe was already loaded with the four packs, and we were ready to set off. He asked, "Just making sure—did you check in with the Mounties' office in Yellowstone and register your plans?"

Holly gave him a look, maybe deciding if she should answer honestly. I knew we never visited a Mountie office, never registered any plans. Holly finally said, "No."

Knute's finger scratched at the empty socket beneath his glasses. "I think that would be a good idea. In fact, it's a requirement."

Holly said, "I think that ship sailed."

Knute shook his head like we didn't understand. I knew the type—responsible, a rule follower, an authoritarian. Jake would not like this guy. He said, "Let me have your names and contact information, and I'll radio in your plans to arrive at Baker Lake in forty days. Then you'll need to check out with the Mountie office there, so they don't start searching for you."

Holly crossed her arms over her chest. "Okay, fine."

Knute asked more questions. "Do you have a satellite phone, a personal locator beacon, bear spray?" I could sense that Knute knew he was pushing it, but he was going to do his duty, cover his tracks in case anything went wrong.

"No sat phone, but I have a PLB with texting capabilities. No bear spray." Her tone was one of annoyance like he was questioning her judgment, maybe questioning her gender, and I was ready to hear him say *missy* or *honey*, but I knew he wouldn't.

He said, "You need to know that two years ago, six boys from the States did the Dubawnt River farther south and had a run-in with a grizzly. They were a month in when one of the boys took a hike alone outside their camp and stumbled upon one. The grizzly took a few false charges, and the kid, like he was supposed to, stood his ground and talked calmly to the bear, talked to it like a dog, 'Good bear, nice bear.' Finally, the bear all-out charged, made a few passes, and each time raked its claws across the kid's face and back. He was down on the ground after that, balled up and playing rag doll to let the bear do what it wanted. It sunk its teeth into the kid's thigh and then started batting him around with its paws as big as catcher's mitts. That was the last thing the boy remembered before going unconscious. He woke up, incredibly still alive, and had to drag his ragged leg back to camp. The boys had packed a satellite phone and they called for help, but they were on a narrow stretch of the river with no space for me to land. They had to paddle the kid sixty miles to a remote Native village where I *could* land. I flew him to the closest hospital, nearly 160 kilometers to Baker Lake.

"I've saved more than one life up here. You need to be careful. I have a spare can of bear spray. Take it, wouldn't want you to end up like that kid on the Dubawnt, trying to talk your way out of a mauling."

Holly took it and said, "Thanks."

He kept on. "I guess you two know what you're getting into, but only ten or so trips go out on the Thelon each season, and half of those come in through the Hanbury, a hundred miles downstream. There's no emergency clinic, no towns or villages, and chances of you seeing another group are unlikely. You sure you know what you're getting into?"

Holly didn't answer immediately. She looked over to him. Her hair was tucked back under the cowboy hat, the one I thought had looked cute but now looked a little foolish, like some pretend tourist. As though she could read my mind, she took it off. She said, "I've made this trip before, three years back. And I'm not living my life buckled into a car seat surrounded by airbags."

Knute smiled. "Neither am I. Over a hundred bush pilots go down each year flying tourists into places they maybe shouldn't go. Sometimes the risks of a remote getaway just aren't worth it."

Holly said, "Sometimes your number comes up. And sometimes, you just lose an eye."

The comment was both serious and funny. I looked up to see Knute's reaction. He blinked his one good eye, then just smiled and repeated, "Sometimes you lose an eye."

I'd relied on Holly to plan the whole trip, to keep us safe, and now I was more than just a little apprehensive. Did Holly know she needed to file some kind of plan? Why hadn't we purchased bear spray or packed a satellite phone? And why hadn't the guy raised all these concerns *before* we took off? And I had more questions: can I take care of myself, rely on myself if I need to?

I knew I could be a little clingy at times, anxious, needy, and dependent, and it looked like I *couldn't* take care of myself. Holly once said I had mommy issues. And that wasn't surprising since I grew up without one. Jake had told me early on that she'd died in childbirth, but I found out later that she just took off after I was born, leaving me with Jake the Snake. I grew up motherless, which, when I did a Google search, meant that I was emotionally impenetrable and careful about choosing the few friends I had. When I did make a friend, I could get a little clingy, which was why Holly sometimes said, "I'm not your mommy." But in all honesty, I didn't think I ever needed a mom, and when push came to shove, I *could* take care of myself, rely on myself. I'd done it before.

Despite all the talk about grizzlies, and heading into a remote wilderness without the comforts of home or medical care, I was feeling pretty fucking lucky. My alternative for the summer was going to be working in Providence, Rhode Island, while everyone I knew—including Holly—took off somewhere else. I probably would've had a job washing dishes and scrubbing pots in some restaurant kitchen. I was lucky to be here, and being in the wilderness was not something I was necessarily scared of. If one of us, or both of us, got hurt or sick, I could deal with it. That's what I thought.

4

We made camp on an island in the middle of the river, a place Holly said would be more bug-free than other spots, but it was still buggy. The blackflies and mosquitoes had been ubiquitous ever since we set foot in northern Canada, merciless in pursuit of warm blood. Holly had bought us bug shirts—the Original Bug Shirt, Elite Edition—in Yellowknife. To ward off bug attacks we could zip up the face netting sewn into the stiff-billed hoods. The blackflies were the worst because they'd find any gap in clothing and burrow in until they found soft flesh. The bites stung, and when I reached in to smash their tiny bodies, trickles of blood would smear on my fingers. Their gouge of the skin left small welts like infected pimples. In the evening, as the sky darkened, mosquitoes would displace the blackflies. They thickened the air like smoke and covered the face netting of my bug shirt so that the world seemed veiled in black lace. The only reprieve from the flies and mosquitoes was a stiff breeze. Holly had said the reason few people came to the Barrens was because of the bugs. This was something I could understand viscerally.

We set up the domed sleeping tent some distance from the bug tent where we planned to cook. The reason being, so Holly said, was that if bears came sniffing around, we'd be far from their path. Inside the bug tent, Holly made a dinner of curried rice and afterward showed me how to wash the dishes without soap by scrubbing them with sand, followed by a rinse in the river. Her camping mantra was, *Leave no trace behind.* I thought this was all very special, this avoidance of polluting the delicate tundra. I was used to the Platte River in Nebraska, thick with algae from farm-leached nitrates and a veritable yard sale of discarded and washed-away garbage that arrived fresh on the riverbanks every spring.

The island was bare of trees, but we did find dry and burnable driftwood along the shore. Holly made a fire below the high-water mark of the Thelon, where the beach stopped and the lichens started. By the following year, any sign of the fire would be washed away by spring floods. The temperature had been in the sixties all day, but with the sun nearing the horizon, it now felt more like forty. The fire was warm against my outstretched hands.

Holly pulled out her pack guitar, an instrument like a ukulele but with a longer neck. We sang a few songs. My favorite was "Wagon Wheel" by Old Crow Medicine Show. Holly liked anything by the Dixie Chicks, and there was a Dylan song I'd also heard Jake play over and over called "Tangled Up in Blue." Holly knew the chords and the words, and she'd taught me how to sing harmony. The wind picked up and the mosquitoes melted away. I pulled off my bug shirt and felt the warmth of the fire on my face. I moved closer to Holly. For a moment we were both quiet, and I reached out to touch her hand. We held hands, and she lifted my fingers to her cheek and then kissed each one. I liked how she did that, unexpected. Just touching felt like hot chocolate warming my insides.

Later she told a story. Holly was an English major and wanted to be a writer, a storyteller. She'd explained that religions were books of stories, that history chronicled stories, and songs told stories. They conformed to an archetype like musical notes—what sounded tonal, emotional—and creating one was as simple as where you came from, your journey, what happened, and what you discovered. Holly wanted her life to read like a collection of unique stories, one adventure after another.

I'd thought about what she said. I hadn't known that living a life of stories was a kind of philosophy—like nihilism, idealism, or Jake's precious anarchism. And I didn't believe that *I* had any personal life philosophy. My motivation was always to get past one obstacle at a time—get out of Nebraska, get to college, get a job, be self-sustaining. Get there and think about all the rest when that time came. But I did feel that my life should be more than just overcoming, that I needed an existential compass of some kind. What Holly said made sense. You needed to create stories throughout your life, a thread that had a narrative to it. And I figured her philosophy needed an *ism*, maybe *storyism*. Holly liked my idea—Holly, the *storyist*.

The story she told was about a kid named Edgar Christian, about the Thelon and the Barren Lands.

"This place hasn't changed in a hundred years, and even back then few paddled the parts of the Thelon where we're going. For white Europeans it was still unexplored territory. But here was where, in the 1920s, a guy named Jack Hornby took two kids roughly our age, Harold Adlard and Edgar Christian, into the

Barrens where all three eventually met their death. The story is known because Edgar left behind a diary detailing what happened.

"At that time in Britain exploring was all the rage. Robert Falcon Scott had reached the South Pole and died on his way back. Robert Peary had reached the North Pole. These guys were like rock stars back home. Edgar grew up reading about their journeys, and John Hornby was his wealthy older cousin who'd explored the Barren Lands. Hornby spent a winter back near Slave Lake with another guy and almost starved to death when he ran out of meat. A year later, he told his story in England and became a legendary explorer in his own right. Edgar, who was just out of school, pleaded with his parents to allow him to go with Jack back to the Barrens.

"What Edgar and his parents didn't know was that Hornby was an odd man and not as capable as he pretended. He and that other guy had almost starved because Hornby was a lousy hunter and didn't pack in enough food for the winter. And over that winter, in the confines of the trapper's shack, they didn't speak to each other for months. In one story I read, the guy almost killed Hornby because he wouldn't go outside in the subzero temperatures to poop.

"Hornby and the two boys got to the Thelon late in the season, September. They quickly built a small cabin in an area that we'll pass by in about two weeks, Hornby Point. It can snow here at any time, and we'll probably see snow before the trip's over, but in September it really starts to snow, and by mid-October the rivers and lakes ice up. They arrived on the Thelon too late to catch the big caribou migration. They needed twenty caribou to get through the winter or one fat moose. He did shoot a few caribou but never found a moose. They had no stores of meat for the winter and by January they were starving.

"We'll see the small cabin, not much bigger than a one-car garage. The three were stuck mostly inside as the temperatures stayed below zero, and the Arctic nights set in with short days and little sunlight. I try to imagine what it was like. I believe under those conditions the core of any relationship would amplify, that some people would grow closer and loving, and some would explode into violence, like the fight over where to defecate. I think that you and I would grow closer. I think we will.

"Anyway, by February, Hornby was dead, followed quickly by Harold. Edgar was left alone in the small cabin trying to live off the hides and bones of the few small animals they'd trapped—he was essentially eating boiled leather. He also dug in the snow for the frozen guts of the fish they'd caught and cleaned the previous fall.

"Edgar was starving. He made it to April when the snow started to melt. In his diary he wrote about a white swan, a whistling swan, flying overhead back to its breeding grounds, and he knew it was spring. The diary ceased for all of May, then one more entry on the first of June. I just remember the one line, 'Weaker than ever, my heart is petering, the sunshine is bright.'

"Before he died, Edgar wrote a last letter to his father and then placed the diary and letter in the stove to protect them from small critters. He also wrote a note: 'Whoever finds this, look in the stove.'

"Two summers later a rescue party was sent out to locate Hornby and the two boys. They found the cabin, the bodies, and the diary. Edgar's father later published the diary. What struck me was the last line in the letter that Edgar wrote, 'I loved Jack like only two men could love each other.' I know that in the confines of that cabin, despite Hornby's eccentricity and ineptitude, the two had grown closer."

As Holly finished her story, she looked up at me and smiled. Did I think we would grow closer while trapped in a small cabin? I'd lived in a small space with Jake, and it was anything but rosy. He told me what to do and I did it—and now I was done with him. I had one other relationship during my first semester, and it was like Jake all over. She told me what to do and I did it, until I didn't. With Holly, our relationship was different. She was the one who took the initiative and had the ideas for where to go and what to do, and I liked that she surprised me, showed me new things—it was exciting—but there was always room for me to say no. I was trying to change, and I'd said no plenty of times. I thought if we were stuck in a tiny cabin in the dead of winter, we'd be accommodating, I'd teach her ways to live and survive, I'd do my pooping outside, and we would grow closer. And I knew that soon, in the confines of the canoe and tent, we'd both find out. What was alarming, though, was that I'd now heard stories of four deaths on the Barrens and one grizzly mauling. And if the pilot hadn't registered our trip with the Mounties, then no one would be looking for us if we didn't arrive at Baker Lake. We'd be found maybe the next season or the season after that—like the three men, like the original owner of the canoe.

I asked, "So why are you taking me here?"

She said, "To grow closer or die trying."

5

Holly steered the canoe onto a rocky beach, and we hiked down the edge of our first set of rapids, all turbulent and scary-looking, Holly scouting for routes.

And what I thought as I looked at the rapids was Jake's favorite line, *Shut the fuck up.* Like when the barometer would drop, and I'd wake up with a throbbing migraine stabbing me between the eyes. When that happened, I could barely get out of bed, wincing and trying to not cry. But it was my job to feed the chickens and collect the eggs before school. If I was running late, Jake would open the door and shout, "Shut the fuck up," and then slam the door so hard it sent a knife blade of pain through my head. I'd get up because he'd conditioned me never to say no and never whine or not do what I was supposed to do. And I was trying not to whine now or tell Holly that I didn't want to do this because it *did* look scary.

The rapids were a cascade of whitewater cutting through sharp rocks and flipping into waves. *Really* scary. Holly's maps were from when she'd taken this trip three years earlier, and there were notes written in pen along the river's length. She'd written the names for the two boulders we needed to avoid, names she'd given them three years back. She said, "The first boulder is Jaws. See the deep water and how it flows like a funnel to the left? That's where we need to go. The hard part is getting back across the river to hit the second boulder, Cherry Bomb, on the right. We'll need to paddle our asses off to get over there. Then we plow through the standing waves below Cherry Bomb where the falling water backs up against the slack current of the river. We need to hit the waves straight on or we'll dump."

I was nodding.

She continued, "There's a rule of whitewater: If one paddler is uncomfortable with the set and says no, then we don't do it, and we portage."

I *was* uncomfortable, and Holly left that quiet space for me to say no, but there was no way I was going to say no. The discomfort I felt was linked to a sense of excitement—I knew this was going to be thrilling. And to myself, I said, *Shut the fuck up.*

To Holly I said, "Let's do it."

Back in the canoe, Holly paddled stern. She showed me again the whitewater strokes to stay off the rocks—the draw, cross draw, and the pry. She said that we had to communicate continually, and we had to yell out the obstacles and strokes—rock right, rock left, draw, pry right, pry left.

I felt like we were tumbling over a waterfall. The river lifted up the canoe and sent us hurtling through a maze of rocks and stands of foaming whitewater. Right away, Holly shouted for the strokes I needed to make and pointed out the smaller rocks to avoid. My movements were all hesitant and jerky but got the job done. I saw the first boulder, Jaws. Holly followed the deeper water as it plummeted to the left. The canoe picked up speed as we dropped. The bow plunged into a trough and spray blasted my face and chest. I shook my head and blinked to clear my vision. I heard Holly say, "Switch," then, "Paddle hard." I shifted my hands, switched my paddle to the other side, and dug in.

It had looked doable from the shore but reaching Cherry Bomb now seemed impossible. I was paddling as hard as I could, the canoe crossing almost perpendicular to the flow of the river. Up close, the boulder had a red quartz sheen, and I could almost touch it. Somehow, we needed to pass on the far side. I didn't think we could make it and envisioned the canoe slammed against the boulder's side, then vised in by the pressure of rushing water that filled the canoe and finally swamping us, sending two bodies along with four packs into the river. Holly yelled, "Cross draw!" I lifted my paddle to the other side and pulled against the water. The bow swung against the current and we ran to the right of Cherry Bomb. The side of the canoe hit rock and I saw the hull dent inward. I waited for it to burst. The hull held and scraped through the turn. The mass of whitewater pushing us was like an avalanche. The canoe launched up with a feeling of weightlessness before plunging into the three-foot standing wave below. We hit it straight on and the canoe filled with gallons of water. I was knocked off my knees and completely soaked.

We hit calm. I felt exhilarated. I lifted my paddle above my head and let out a loud, "Yes, yes." I looked behind and Holly joined me, yelling, whooping. The feeling was like nothing I'd experienced before, and Holly was looking back at me, smiling, and I thought she liked that she had taken me on this roller-coaster ride—that I thought it was awesome.

At that moment I loved her for bringing me here.

THAT NIGHT WE lay side by side in our sleeping bags zipped together, silent. I was exhausted from the day's excitement and exertion. I could hear the river in the distance and the soft wind that sounded like leaves rustling against the tent wall. I felt comfortable in our isolation and solitude. I wanted sleep but also something else. It'd been over a week since we'd had sex, and my body craved the feeling of release. I faced her and held her close. I felt her warm breath on my nose and cheeks and then on my ear, and she softly kissed my ear. Then our mouths met. Holly had plump lips and kissing her was soft and wet. My body reacted and our kissing became more passionate—tongues and teeth.

I wasn't experienced, and sex with Holly was a new feeling of total absorption. Over time our sex had changed and evolved. She pushed me to understand what I liked, told me what she liked. At first the dialogue was uncomfortable, but eventually I learned to enjoy the exploration of senses that followed. Sex now was a give-and-take of touches, sensations, excitement, and pleasure. Our movements became a musical improvisation founded on past patterns.

6

We walked inland with our P-packs to find a tent site on the tundra. Shrubs sat on a layer of stagnant swamp water just above the permafrost, a breeding ground for mosquitoes. We both wore our knee-high neoprene Muck Boots that sunk ankle-deep in the soupy mixture, making a sucking sound. We kept walking, moving up a gradual slope to find dry ground. The spot we chose was on an outcrop of flat granite covered by crunchy sage-colored caribou lichen and interspersed with soft peat moss in shades of orange and green.

We couldn't find driftwood for a fire, so we cooked in the bug tent on our single-burner camp stove. The sky was cloudless, and we left off the rain canopy. The bugs covered the netting and surrounded us with their loud drone, creating a vulnerable caged feeling like we were exotic zoo animals to be observed and considered.

During dinner we talked, or rather Holly talked. She described our route the next day and what to expect. I sat and listened, asking the few obligatory questions that kept the conversation going, providing the prompts to show I was paying attention. But as she talked, I thought back through what she'd told me of her past. I knew she'd grown up spending summers on canoeing trips with other kids and counselors from Camp Kawishiwi. She'd canoed this same route along the Thelon with three other girls. She lived in her own apartment off-campus. She'd had other girlfriends at college but no one steady or serious. She never talked about past girlfriends or boyfriends in high school. I knew her parents were wealthy and paid for almost anything she wanted. She'd grown up in Saint Paul, in Minnesota, with its northern border touching Canada and Lake Superior.

After Holly finished with her plan for the next day, I asked her, "Why didn't we go through Saint Paul on our trip here?" I thought then that maybe Holly didn't want her family to meet me.

"I just did the Google map and the northern route was faster." She sat across from me in the tent with the stove and food between us. She looked up as she said this and then reached over to scoop more pasta onto her plate. Casual, like no big deal.

"You didn't want your family to know about me. Is that right?"

"No, that's not right."

Then I realized what the hang-up was, and I just said it, "Your parents don't know you're gay, do they?"

She took her time to answer. She looked ready to cry. She said, "No, they don't.'

I asked, "Why?" The tone I used was sympathetic and soft, not accusatory. I honestly wanted to know. I assumed her parents were educated, probably liberal, probably understanding. Coming out shouldn't have been a big deal.

"I have a story to tell. It's embarrassing."

"Okay."

Holly set her plate down, wiped at her eyes that had begun to tear, then sat upright, composing herself to speak.

"You know my family has money, but I haven't told you their story. My dad comes from this old wealthy Saint Paul family. His grandfather was a lumber baron who clear-cut most of northern Minnesota. There's a hall at the university named after him, from donating a bunch of money, and a city street carries our family name. My mom married into Dad's family and took on her role as a kind of society Brahmin. She's stodgy conservative Saint Paul, maybe politically progressive but conservative in everything else. She's on the board of the orchestra and a past president of the Junior League. She wears a helmet of hair like Margaret Thatcher. You know, all high hair with a flip, stiff as a Tupperware bowl. She's overtly behind the gay community—she watches *Ellen* and *Oprah*—but covertly not in her family, not on her watch. Part of me just doesn't want to burst her bubble.

"I had a crush on a girl in seventh grade who was all tomboyish and cool. Her name was Tonya. We became friends. I was learning the guitar, and Tonya was a good singer. We'd hang out in her bedroom or mine and play music and talk. Then one afternoon, I reached out and touched her hand. It was electric, like we were meant to touch. Minutes later we were making out. I was in heaven. I went home that night exhilarated but also scared. I knew I liked other women, but I thought maybe it was normal, like we all imagined how beautiful and cool it would be to make out with Natalie Portman or Pink, like for sure you'd do it given the chance. But I felt that kissing Tonya had somehow been taboo, that I'd crossed a line. Then I did a stupid thing—I stopped seeing Tonya and ignored her in school. I could tell she felt sad and alone, and betrayed. Then I did betray her. I started telling other girls she was gay and had come on to me. I did that shitty thing. Tonya wasn't outwardly bullied or teased after that, but she was ignored. People just stopped talking to her, and then she got all withdrawn and silent. Tonya sat by herself in the lunchroom and walked alone, avoided, in the hallways. Before the year ended, she transferred to a public school, and I rarely saw her again. And if I did see her at the mall or getting ice cream, we'd ignore each other like neither existed. I betrayed her.

"Then, at home one night, my mom asked if I knew about my friend Tonya. It was odd, I remember my mom was wearing her fur coat inside, one that was probably stitched together from forty mink pelts. She wore that coat inside around the house but never outside where she might be PETA-shamed. She asked me about Tonya and I lied. I said that I hadn't heard anything but that I knew she wasn't happy at the academy and transferred. My mom said she'd heard Tonya had a nervous breakdown and that she was gay, and did I know she was gay? I said I had no clue. Then my mom came right out and said that her mother must be so embarrassed. Embarrassed! That's when I knew—not in her family, not on her watch. I'm still scared to tell them. It's fucked-up, I know it. I never had the guts to come out. And I live this private shadowy life outside of Saint Paul. Why is that? Why can't I just tell her I'm gay? It's the fucking twenty-first century. Maybe it's just easier to keep secrets, let her fantasies live. Like why would you tell a dying woman that she was putting on weight?"

I said, "That's a fucked-up analogy."

"I know. My mother's not dying of anything, and I'm sure she won't die of humiliation. I'll tell her when we get back."

I asked, "What *did* you tell them?"

"I told them I was going back to the Thelon with my friend Lee."

"So, they think I'm a guy?"

"Yes."

I let that piece of information settle. It was fucked-up and embarrassing, embarrassing for both of us, and I knew I could point a finger, look for some kind of reckoning, but it wasn't that easy. I didn't think anyone wanted to be gay, to be different. I knew my life would have been, would be, so much easier if I were straight. I'd probably have a whole group of high school friends, I'd have gone on dates and maybe had a boyfriend people liked, gone to dances and the prom, and I wouldn't be so emotionally fucked-up. I wouldn't have guys like that pilot, Knute, looking at me funny. I wouldn't have future employers guessing if I'd be some workplace liability. I could tell it was also difficult for Holly, probably heart-wrenching, and she didn't need me piling on. I needed to take what she'd said at face value, and I knew Holly would come out to her parents when she was ready.

What I did say was, "Well, that's *really* fucked-up. You're like this person who hides who she really is—a withholder, a hider."

She said again, "I know."

7

The Barrens were the same moonscape as the day before—hilly eskers formed by retreating glaciers that snaked alongside the river, sandbars that turned the water emerald green or chlorine blue, stunted black spruce sprouting from granite cracks, the tundra with its carpet of caribou lichen like desert camo. I pointed out a small flower, pink on a thick stubby shrub almost like a cactus. I said, "Alpine azalea." Holly had no clue.

We turned a bend and saw a grizzly and dead musk ox. The grizzly lay dozing on the beach, and as we moved closer saw or smelled us, and stood tall on its rear legs. The bear's fur was bleached auburn and its enormous head spanned the width of its shoulders—a male. His thick arms hung down with claws pointed inward, long and curved like meat hooks. And now I could smell the rot of the musk ox, like sulfur and dung. I was more awed than scared. The grizzly stood, watching, I guessed wondering if we were prey or predator. I knew he could swim, but I also figured he'd had his fill of meat—he was probably more scared than hungry. He finally dropped to all fours and lumbered off in the opposite direction. On the shore was the half-eaten musk ox, its head and horns parting the water like a rock in the current. One eye was clouded and looked inward, and the other was just a messy hole of flesh. Holly took out her solar-charged iPhone and took photos. A raven came from seemingly nowhere and landed near the corpse. It stepped cautiously closer and stretched its long beak to rip off a strip of carrion.

Later, in deeper water, I looked down past my paddle and saw the topside of a lake trout twisting into the current. That evening I put together the fishing rod and tied my smallest #8 hook with two beads of the salmon eggs we carried for bait. I let the line drift into a hole on the inside turn of the river. I took one smaller trout the length of my forearm that I cleaned far from camp, leaving the scraps for bears or wolves or ravens. Despite the returning blackflies, we cooked the trout sprinkled with salt over a driftwood fire. My body must've been starved for fresh protein, because I told Holly it was the best fish I'd ever tasted.

After dinner we searched for more driftwood and built a fire. The smoke chased away the flies and we took off our bug shirts. Holly played her guitar. One song, "Travelin' Soldier," was about a guy who never came home from the war in Vietnam, and the girl who was left to remember him—a *love that would never die*. . . . Holly played it mournful and slow, and though I'm not usually a sucker for music and lyrics, I found myself almost crying.

Then Holly said, "It's time *you* tell a story about yourself. You've never told me what it was like growing up in Nebraska, what your father thinks of you, who your father really is. Maybe you're a hider just like me. So, tell me a story. And start from the beginning, where you came from, the journey, what happened, and what you discovered."

So, I did. I started from the beginning, where we lived, details I'd avoided telling Holly in the past, details I was embarrassed about, that I thought made me seem like some survivalist freak, which I probably was. I told her the story about how Jake made me track a deer I'd poached on our property in Nebraska.

"Our farm didn't have your typical house, more like a piece of one, really just the basement. Jake had bought it that way. The house was on ten acres of land just outside the small city of Columbus. The property bordered a state forest that stretched into a thousand-acre bend of the Platte River, land that flooded just about every spring. Jake bought the place right before I was born. The property came cheap. The previous owner had run out of money after the foundation was built, then just laid a flat roof over the basement. It looked like a bunker, and that's what we called it, the bunker. You walked down a flight of stairs to enter, and inside was a large room with a kitchen, table and chairs, a sofa, and a rocker. Along the wall were two sculling oars from the seventies, from when Jake won a race at the Head of the Charles in Boston. Jake's bedroom was in the back, and my room was a large alcove, probably planned for storing canned goods. We had running water pumped by an old windmill that filled an above-ground tank, but we had no toilet and crapped in an outhouse. There was no city electricity. We cooked on a propane stove and had a small refrigerator made for an RV that mostly stored Jake's home-brewed beer. There were a few egress windows for daylight, and at night the place was lit with LED lights strung from a pile of twelve-volt batteries charged by a solar panel on the roof. We had a vegetable garden, chickens, and a few goats. We hunted deer, rabbits, squirrels, muskrats, and ducks along the river. We fished. Jake was into the eco-anarchist movement, the whole Tolstoy, Thoreau, Zerzan back-to-nature thing. Jake said that he'd heard John Zerzan speak one time in Eugene, Oregon, and he claimed it changed his life. Jake would say things to me like, 'We can either passively go down the road to servitude and destruction or turn in the direction of a feral life.' I can remember all the stuff Jake said because he said it over and over, and I had to listen. He hated civilization and technology, and hated money, and he wanted to live off the land as much as possible.

"One evening in July, we were driving back from town along the dirt road through our property. It was hot, and we knew that deer came to the road to get away from the flies, and we were low on meat. We drove slowly and saw a doe standing in buckthorn just off to the side. Jake inched along in our pickup. He kept a Smith & Wesson .38 revolver on him almost always. The deer stood stock-still and Jake gave me the gun. The sun was just down and still dusky so I could see just fine. Jake liked to use the old-fashioned word *gloaming*, the time right after sunset when the horizon was still lit but the darkness of night hadn't descended.

"I saw the doe standing there about twenty feet into the woods. I took my shot. A .38 doesn't have much stopping power with a deer, so I went for the head. The deer dropped. We got out of the pickup and walked into the woods. I still had the gun in my hand, and I was ready to take another shot if the deer lay just wounded. Then as I got closer, I fucking tripped over a fallen branch. The deer was only wounded and now spooked. It jumped up and ran off just as I tried to take another shot. And now Jake looked at me as though I was some kind of idiot. He said, 'Everything in the world is moved by an inner urge to become something greater than it is.' Which was his way of saying, *Shut the fuck up and go get it.*

"I followed the doe into the state forest. I knew I'd hit her somewhere around the head or neck but not in the vitals and not in the brainpan. I walked the trail slowly, methodically following the blood trail. In the shadow of that gloaming light color appears as shades of gray, and what I followed was the glimmering moisture of the blood stuck to leaves. A lot of blood, so I figured the deer would be dead in one or two hours. And I knew a wounded deer would be thirsty and probably head toward water.

"I followed the blood trail until it was just too dark. I headed in the direction the deer was heading, southwest, away from town and toward the river. I used the new moon as my guide. A couple of times I heard a rustle, and I followed that. And each time, the sound kept pulling me toward the river. It was past midnight when I finally reached the water. I could hardly see a thing, and it was quiet and I figured the deer was dead somewhere along the river, but I couldn't find her. And I wasn't going back to the bunker without the deer. So, I just curled up and fell asleep.

"I woke up with the rising sun and started looking again. I was thirsty, but you didn't drink water from the Platte, and I was still tired but I wouldn't go back to get Jake. I kept looking. Within a couple hours, I found the doe, dead. She was just off the river lying down in a stand of reeds like she'd gone to sleep. Now I needed to carry the hundred-pound deer to the bunker, two or three miles back through the woods.

"I always kept a folding knife on me, the same one I have now. I went to work field-dressing the deer. This will gross you out, but I sliced off pieces of the heart and ate them raw for breakfast. The carcass now was about only seventy-five pounds, and I carried that bloody thing across my shoulders for the next hour and a half it took to stumble home. And there stood Jake, waiting and smiling. I flipped the carcass down at his feet. I was pissed by then. He could have come looking for me—he could have helped. All he needed to do was call out, and I probably would have heard him and returned his call. It wasn't easy hauling a heavy piece of meat with bones and limbs and hooves and head. He could have helped. But I knew he wouldn't. For Jake, it was always some kind of test. And he's always going to let you know it was a test. He said, 'Everything in the world moves naturally to a specific fulfillment.'

"Well, fuck."

Holly stirred the coals and took it all in. I'd told her selected details about my home and upbringing. I didn't lie, but the gaps were staggering—I *was* a hider. I would eventually, though, tell Holly my whole twisted story.

Then she asked if Jake molested or hurt me in any way, and I said to her that Jake would never do that, he wasn't that kind of freak.

She asked, "Truthfully?"

I looked up to meet her eyes. I said, "Yes, truthfully."

My life, though, wasn't all sunshine and rainbows. While in college, I did a Google search that turned up the ten-question online survey for Adverse Childhood Experiences, ACE, a predictor of physical and emotional problems. I took it.

Was I insulted, sworn at? *Yes.* Was I often slapped or pushed or grabbed? *No.* Was I touched sexually by an adult? *Yes.* Did I feel unloved? *No.* Did I feel there wasn't enough food or clean clothes? *No.* Was I from a broken family? *Yes.* Was I kicked or slapped by my mother? *No.* Did I live with someone who used street drugs? *Yes.* Was my father depressed or mentally ill? I would say *Yes.* Did someone go to prison? *Yes.* So that was an ACE score of five with a five times higher likelihood that I'd have problems with anxiety, depression, suicide, drug abuse, weight, and a host of other issues. Check, check, check, check, and check.

Holly said, "I'd like to meet Jake sometime."

I just smiled. I didn't tell her that Jake was in prison, and meeting him was unlikely. I didn't tell her that he was kind of an asshole.

8

On the map Holly pointed out the railroad track marks that indicated rapids. The next stretch of the river was covered in tracks along with her notes. A few we could run, some we'd need to portage, some we could line. Holly kept the current map folded in one pocket of her life vest, which also carried the PLB that clipped to the meshed fabric. Before we set off for the day, she showed me what our route would be. By tomorrow she wanted to camp at the falls near Jim Lake. Then three or four days to the Thelon Canyon and a four-mile portage, the longest of the trip.

We ran three sets of rapids without pausing to scout them first. Holly called out the strokes that I then delivered. The game of dodge-the-rocks was exciting and unlike anything I'd experienced. The adrenaline rush tensed all my muscles and senses so that shooting the rapids became all-consuming like a drug, and I found myself wanting more. I loved it and never said no.

More rapids were ahead. We scouted most, portaged twice, and lined once. Scouting was a chess game of if-we-do-this, or if-we-do-that, and I found myself arguing with Holly and trying to figure out a way down every set. Holly leaned toward caution, avoiding rapids that could dump us into the river or worse, which I knew was the right thing to do. But of course, now I was a whitewater junkie and couldn't help myself. And to be honest, portaging sucked—unpacking and packing, hauling all four packs and the canoe, humping all that across uneven ground. Lining was a little more interesting. We strung our rope through the canoe, tying off at the loops on the bow and stern. Holly went first, stepping from rock to rock along the shore and guiding the bow and yelling back commands. I was behind, probably because I was big, an anchor. I held the line to the stern and slowly walked the canoe downriver like a dog on a leash. The process was slow, the footing slippery and treacherous, but anything was better than portaging.

Later in the day a cairn marked one of the longer portages. Onshore, the blackflies swarmed, and we zipped up our bug shirts before unloading the packs. Holly lifted the canoe to her thighs with a hand on each gunwale. With a quick jerk, she swung the canoe up onto her shoulders, the weight eased by the padded yoke. Her thin legs stuck out from under the canopy of the canoe, I thought, like toothpicks in a hot dog. She started up the path and I lifted a food pack onto my shoulders and followed. Our portage paralleled the river, and Holly stopped to point out a ledge in the rapids followed by a shadowed hole where the water curled back on itself. She said that if we'd continued paddling, and we got caught in that hole, the canoe would've likely been swamped and pinned there by the backflow of water. Then the force of the water would've pressed us down and under, tumbling our bodies like clothes in a washer until the current finally spit us out—probably drowned and dead. On the second trip I carried the other food pack and Holly carried both P-packs, one strapped to her back and the other strapped to her chest. Holly weighed maybe 120 pounds, so she was humping more than her own weight.

We took a rest halfway along the portage near a small lake and sat against a sandstone ledge that overlooked the tundra. I spotted spring flowers along the lake's shore. They spread out in small islands of color against the green tundra and were no larger than a quarter, most dime-sized. I tried to put a name to each one, names I'd nearly memorized through Google searches before we'd left. I pointed them out to Holly—Indian paintbrush with narrow scarlet petals, a pink star shape I thought was primrose, wild violet rhododendron, yellow varieties of cinquefoil, and a field of tall-stemmed purple lupines. I showed her a cluster of Labrador tea shrubs with bunches of small white flowers at the head of leafed stalks. The tea from the shrubs was like a catch-all herbal remedy for coughs, lung infections, diarrhea, and sore muscles. The names and information rattled off my tongue like some text-to-speech voice generator. It was my anxious form of relaxation, like a jigsaw puzzle or game of solitaire.

Holly pulled out a bag of trail mix and offered it to me. I took a handful and passed it back. Then she told me to close my eyes. She said that when I opened them, I shouldn't try to focus on any one thing, just let my eyes take it all in without examination. I did what she said, and then stared unfocused at the landscape of lake, flowers, sky, and endless tundra. Holly said it was like music, one note meant nothing, but the melody of notes strung together could be totally emotional, sublime. *Sublime*, it was another of the old-fashioned words Jake liked to use. He'd define it as a kind of moral high ground, a level of spiritual purity, and his usage eventually struck me as bullshit. I thought what Holly meant was more like beauty or inspiration. Holly said, "Keep looking and don't focus and don't think about anything and try to still your body and your mind."

I knew she knew I couldn't do this. It reminded me of a time when I was about eight. Jake had this book about telekinesis by Uri Geller, and I tried for weeks to move a spoon across a table with my mind. I tried hard, concentrating all my thoughts toward that one objective. I even brought home a plastic spoon to test my powers on something lighter. I could never get that spoon to move. Then it turned out Uri Geller was nothing more than an illusionist and liar. But I tried to do as Holly said. I looked at the entire landscape without focusing on any one thing. I could feel my mind trying to shift gears—I knew what it did, I wasn't unfamiliar with its workings.

Holly said, "Focus on your breathing and slow it to where it's just barely feeding your body."

Holly was trying to get me to meditate, still my anxiety, without using the word *meditate*. She was into that sort of thing—yoga, reflexology, acupuncture. I relaxed, looked at the entire landscape, pushed out my intruding thoughts, and focused on my steady breathing. And I did feel the wind touching my cheeks, and for a second, I saw how the same wind was moving everything in waves across the tundra. And then at the edge of my vision I caught the movement of some small animal. I saw the grayish fur of its tail, its pointed ears, and instinctively said out loud, "A fox."

Holly said, "At least you tried."

9

We came across two tundra swans, all white with black beaks. As we approached, they kick-paddled downriver away from our canoe, but stopped as we closed the distance. Then they flapped their wings, a span of four feet or more, and danced along the water to get elevation. Their wings made a whistling noise as the air was displaced, and I remembered Edgar in Holly's story seeing a whistling swan. It had been spring and right before he died. Around the next bend, the two swans were there again. For three turns in the river we played out the same pantomime, and it began to feel as though we were being teased along, lured in—a fatal trap just around the corner. Finally, they took flight for the last time and were gone.

The river narrowed as we approached the falls, and Holly pulled off on the right side. In the distance I could see the walls of a gorge rise above the river, and I knew this portage was going to be a bitch. A cairn marked a trail, but there was no trail to speak of, just rocks, ledges, and boulders. We unloaded the packs and Holly helped lift the canoe up and onto my shoulders—it was my turn to hump it. We started climbing, and I chose my footing carefully among the shifting rocks. Once I stumbled and dropped the canoe. I said, "Shit," and Holly said, "Fuck," but the canoe was made of a thick plastic-like compound and almost indestructible. It bounced and slid down the hill, banging against rocks. Holly looked at me like the idiot I was, like don't do that again. I hiked down and started over.

On our first trip across we took a rest and walked to the gorge's edge. The falls were impressive, sending the contents of the Thelon down sixty feet of rock. The mist rushed up, chasing away the blackflies and coating us like dew.

By the end of the day the few trees we'd been seeing vanished, and we moved into a part of the Barren Lands entirely devoid of them—truly barren. We camped on a pebble-strewn beach with lichens and blooms of moss covering the rocks as far as the eye could see. We found driftwood where the whitewater of the falls emptied into a pool formed by an eddy. Before dinner, we swam in the pool and did our best to clean our bodies without soap. The water was ice-cold and we didn't linger. After dinner, we lit a fire. The breeze and smoke kept away most of the bugs.

I asked Holly to tell a story. Make one up, something that happens in the future, maybe with us.

It took her a while to think through each part of the story, then she began.

"We live in a small one-and-a-half story bungalow in Minneapolis. Even though you're a famous mathematician, you enjoy working with wood and doing things with your hands. You've redone the woodwork of our bungalow and have built out the second story with a bathroom for our son, who's turning fourteen and needs his own space. I'm a writer and have just published my second book, another novel set in the Barrens. I teach writing at the local college. We have a life together and, believe it or not, we're happy. I'm happy, even though you make way more money than I do.

"We'd decided to have a family—we both always wanted a child, one child. We couldn't screw our way into pregnancy, so we found a donor from the sperm bank at the university. All we knew was that the donor was a college professor from somewhere in the Midwest, had a genius IQ, was six foot tall, weighed 180 pounds, and was of southern European descent with black hair. I carried the baby, and the child was born with a full head of black hair and my green eyes. We named him Theo after the Thelon. From the beginning, we knew he was brilliant, and by the age of five, he could play my guitar better than I did. He wrote his first song, called, 'Mommies in the Kitchen,' and it sounded a lot like, 'I've Been Working on the Railroad.' He did well in a gifted and talented program and was nervous about starting public high school.

"Theo loves both of us, we're his family, but he also wants to know who his father is. We'd been honest with him, a sperm donor who wished to remain anonymous. All we had was a profile, and we shared that with him. But Theo is smart. Without telling us, he gets his DNA tested at Ancestry.com. His DNA points him toward a Spanish family line with the surname of Noya, and through the internet he tracks the Noyas from Zaragoza in northern Spain to the Midwest. There were more Noyas than you might think, and Theo starts calling each one. He's looking for a Noya who's a college professor. He finds only one, his father, and writes the man a letter. Theo admits that his reasons for wanting to meet are as mysterious to him as they must be to the professor. It comes down to this: to know himself, he needs to know where he came from—much of the self is comprised of genetics. And the professor gets that, so he writes back saying, yes, he would welcome a visit and he'll be in Minneapolis later in the summer to meet with colleagues. His name is Oscar Noya. They plan to meet at a coffee shop. Theo has told none of this to us, his mothers.

"Theo rides his bike to the coffee shop a half hour before the planned meeting. He orders a caramel macchiato and sits down at a table he thinks will allow some privacy and watches the door. He thinks his father will be punctual, wear a sports coat, and have a close-trimmed beard. And he's right. At the appointed minute, a man walks through the door. He's six feet tall and wears a blue sports coat over a starched white shirt. His black hair is peppered gray at the temples, and his beard is solid gray. Theo notices all this. The man, Oscar Noya, instantly recognizes Theo, who stands up as the man walks to the table. They shake hands and Theo sees the man's smile, but it seems off somehow—not quite sincere. They sit down, and his father does not order coffee. Theo is nervous and lets the man ask all the questions. Theo reveals the details of his life: friends, music, high school, two mothers. The thought of two mothers stops the man—I guess he hadn't considered that possibility, like maybe he thought he was helping a husband with fertility problems. He repeats, 'two mothers,' and Theo says our names, 'Holly and Lee.' Oscar says that he teaches developmental psychology and that he understands the statistics regarding a fatherless child, that there's a high likelihood of drug or alcohol abuse, poverty, anger, and other antisocial issues. He asks a series of diagnostic questions: had Theo ever done drugs or tried alcohol, does he have trouble fitting in at school? Theo then notices the professor's eyebrows are sculpted and dyed black, and the joints in the man's hand pop with arthritis, and he's thinking, *Who is this creepy old guy?* And Theo, not wanting to insult the man he just met, and trying to be polite, just says that he isn't fatherless, he just has two mothers, that his family is intact and he's doing fine—Theo doesn't answer the man's questions. There's an awkward silence, and finally, Oscar Noya excuses himself and says he has another appointment to attend. Theo then rides his bike home.

"And that's it, a brief meeting and a pedantic guy, a psychology professor, telling our son that he has a high probability of drug abuse and antisocial behavior.

"Later that night Theo comes clean to both of us and tells the story of finding his biological father. And you ask Theo if he liked his father, and did he want to meet him again? Theo says, 'No.' He didn't think he liked the man and, no, he didn't think he would like to meet him again. And then he says, 'I don't have to be my father.'

"That touched both of us, especially you."

Holly was finished with her story. I *was* touched, touched that she imagined our lives entwined, that she'd thought about the possibility of being together and having a family. I never trusted the future, and I desperately wanted to believe that the two of us might have one together.

10

For the next three days the river moved in gentle curves through the sand and gravel banks of the Thelon. My hands were killing me, and I continually readjusted my grip to avoid the spots where my skin was ready to blister. It seemed stupid we didn't bring gloves, and I asked Holly why. She said, "You can't get a good grip with gloves, and your hands will sweat, and you'll just make them worse. Don't hold your paddle in a death grip, but don't relax too much either." She added, "Blisters are inevitable. You'll just have to tough it out until calluses form."

And that was something I knew how to do—tough it out.

At the end of three days we camped on an island that was formed as the Thelon moved into two channels and emptied into Eyeberry Lake. It had been over a week since we left Yellowknife.

Around the fire Holly asked about Jake, if he was a good father, if I loved him, and I told her a story.

"Jake was stuck, he'd made his choices. He'd decided before I was born, maybe while he was still in college, that he wasn't going to live a conventional life and he wasn't going to take a paycheck.

He said that most people were slaves to a system that breaks down the spirit. He didn't want to be part of that system, so he bought the place on the river and fashioned it into something that could provide most of the food and shelter we needed. He bartered for things he couldn't grow or build himself. He worked under the table for the cash needed to pay property taxes and stuff we had to buy from stores. He also grew and sold some weed. He tried to live what he thought was a life outside the system. Of course, there were cracks in his utopian vision and compromises he accepted. An emergency room couldn't turn him away if he or I became injured with a broken bone or infection. Later, Jake collected food stamps. But under the circumstances, Jake lived the life he aspired to.

"I think Jake probably wanted a boy to follow in his footsteps, but what he got was me. Regardless, as far as he was concerned, I was going to follow in his footsteps. He had his lessons that started before I could even remember, lessons about his anarchist philosophy but also about things like repairing an engine, hunting, fixing a broken ax, processing goat meat, and, yes, carpentry. He thought schools were indoctrination centers and wouldn't have allowed me to go if the county hadn't forced him to enroll me.

"It was hard for Jake to let me out of his sight. While I was still in grammar school, he'd walk me to the end of our driveway to catch the bus, and he'd be there in the afternoon when the bus dropped me off. I did my homework, but Jake didn't care one way or the other about test scores or grades. Maybe he hoped I'd flunk out one day. But I studied obsessively. I didn't fit in socially—I never belonged to any clique of girls, and for years I didn't feel comfortable around anyone my age. So, I think studying was my way of distancing myself from other kids. That and my weight. Anyway, I always got As.

"I was close to one teacher in high school—she taught math. Her name was Lonnie Longfellow. That was her real, married name as far as I know. She was big and butch looking. Her hair was cut short, a crew cut, and iron-gray. She wore men's clothes—Levi's, flannels buttoned up to her throat, brown oxford shoes. Her glasses were the kind engineers wear, or hipsters if you're in Providence, and I think everyone just assumed she was gay. But she lived south of the river on a farm with a husband and four kids. I thought she sensed I was gay, and maybe we were kindred spirits. Maybe she had empathy and wanted to guide me through my shitty high school years. She'd give me books to read, two or three at a time, and I'd consume them like some kids read comics. A few changed my life and steered me toward math. One inspired me, *The Man Who Knew Infinity*, about a dirt-poor kid from India who ended up creating breakthrough mathematical theories at Oxford. By my junior year Lonnie was lending me ten books at a time, often stuff the local libraries didn't carry, books about mathematics but also classics like Aristotle, the Bible, fiction and nonfiction literature, memoirs, and biographies. I'd later see her basement study lined with books by the thousands.

"She was the one who helped me apply for college when I'd finally decided to get out of Columbus. I told her that Jake and his father, my grandfather, had gone to Brown. She said I had the grades, almost perfect SAT scores, and that being a legacy applicant counted. Lonnie thought I could get in. She helped me fill out the forms and gave me feedback on my essay. She said that a letter to the school from my father and grandfather would help. She said that she'd talk to Jake.

"I was reluctant and conflicted. I did love Jake. He was more than just my father; he was my only family, really all I had. And I knew Jake wouldn't let me go easily. Jake heard her car in the driveway and heard the door open and close and heard the footsteps. Few people ever came to visit. I was in the bunker with him, and we waited for the knock. Jake opened the door and just said, 'What?' She asked to come in, and Jake said, 'Why?' I yelled at Jake to just let her in, and he stepped aside. She sat down at our kitchen table and I sat down with her. Jake remained standing. She told Jake that she'd been working with me on a college application. She asked for his help and understanding.

"I didn't know that Lonnie would unexpectedly come to the property. And I can only imagine what she thought of the basement where I lived. Jake was silent after she said her piece. Now I was scared because Jake didn't know I had applied to college, and I think it never occurred to him that I would leave. He was staring at Lonnie, and I didn't know what he was thinking. I said, 'Thanks Lonnie, I'll see you on Monday at school.' I got her out of the place as fast as possible before Jake exploded. And then he did. He threw a kitchen chair against the cinderblock wall and overturned the table. I ran into my alcove room that had a curtain for a door and crawled into my bed. I wasn't scared that he'd beat me or hurt me, he wasn't that way. I just needed to give him the space to blow off steam. Finally, he left the bunker. I heard our old Ford pickup start and then roll off the property.

"I didn't see him for days. He'd done this before, and I never knew where he went. I assumed it had something to do with sex—better others than me. It was over a week before he came back. What he had with him was a letter, and he placed it down in front of me on the kitchen table that I'd since repaired. Then he left. The letter had a handwritten name on the envelope, my name. It was from my grandfather, who I'd never met. It said, *I'm very pleased that you're applying. I've sent the dean a letter of recommendation. If what Jake tells me is true, you can be assured of your acceptance. Looking forward to meeting you when you're out east, maybe for Easter.* There was his name, a phone number, and an address in Connecticut. I reread the short letter over and over, trying to find a nuance, any indication of what it might also mean. An hour later Jake came back into the bunker, picked up the letter, and ripped it into confetti. So that was Jake. But he knew I would remember every word, including my grandfather's address."

Holly was quiet and thinking through what I'd said. There was still more I wanted to tell her, but I thought it was best to dole out each story slowly, let Holly absorb them over time so that her judgment of me could be more nuanced, and perhaps less harsh. She touched my wrist and then my hand. We were holding hands and just feeling the warmth of the fire.

I tried to think about the choices I had before me and the stark contrast with where I came from. In Nebraska I'd had the bunker, the animals, the Platte River, the task of working to eat, and my life with Jake that offered nothing in the future that I could visualize for *myself.* Lonnie helped change all that. I had college now, and Holly, and I felt I had more choices. I tried to codify the choices, categorize and name them like I would a landscape of flowers—I could be a carpenter, I could be a college professor, I could be a mathematician, I could manage a business, I could be an engineer, I could go back to Nebraska, I could be with Holly, I could be a wife, I could be a mother, I could have a child named Theo, I could live on my own. And each choice, each decision, redefined who I was and then limited my choices. I didn't dare tell Holly any of this because it was endless and she'd think I was crazy, and she'd tell me I could be all those things. But that wasn't something I knew.

In the morning the sun was high above the horizon, and the light streaked through the fabric of our tent, warming it like a hothouse. As I lay there beside Holly, clouds moved in and covered the harsh sunlight. The temperature in the tent dropped to where it was comfortable, and I wanted to fall back asleep. But then I felt pressure build in my sinuses, the barometer dropping, the weather changing—a storm coming from somewhere.

11

We paddled the length of Eyeberry Lake, and by evening we were back on the twisting Thelon. My head pounded continually, and it was all I could do to keep paddling. Holly steered us toward a protected inlet, where we stopped to camp and hope the storm would pass.

We hiked through the swampy tundra up to a ridge overlooking the Thelon. Farther down was a natural head-high shelf where the ground was dry and flat. In the lee of the shelf was a fire ring made of soot-black rocks. Holly said the camp was hundreds of years old, probably Dene hunters that were here before the Inuit. She said they followed the caribou migrations across the Barrens, and she'd seen other camps like these along the Thelon. Rocks the size of human heads dotted the ground in ring patterns and had most likely been used to hold down the skirts of caribou-hide tents. The site was ancient, and I was awed by their audacity to survive in this wilderness. Maybe they had canoes, but they didn't carry packs of food or stoves to cook. They ate what they killed and killed enough to last through most winters. Still, many died young.

Holly brushed her hand through the firepit and found something she was looking for, a broken flint arrowhead. She showed it to me, just the notched stem that would've been lashed to the wood shaft of an arrow, though it was missing the sharpened point. Jake and I had hunted with a bow and arrow, mostly off-season when we didn't want to exactly shout our intentions to the authorities. It wasn't easy. You couldn't just stalk the deer, like when you hunt with a high-powered rifle, because you couldn't get close enough to hit your prey with the arrow's approximate forty-yard range. You had to wait near a deer trail, usually in a tree stand, until the animal came to you, and then it was still hard as fuck.

I took the arrowhead from Holly, touched its sharp edge, then brought it to my nose. I thought I could smell the animal fats that had soaked in over the countless years. I tried to imagine how it had ended up in the fire. Probably the hunter sat nearby, striking at the flint with a hammerstone, maybe too forcefully, until, *snap*, the point broke. The pissed-off hunter then tossed the remnants into the fire.

We set up camp while the wind continued to blow. My headache was constant, and I washed down three aspirins from the first-aid kit. The pain moved from the stabbing between my eyes to a dull throb. The wind direction changed to the west, and that evening we watched darker clouds drift in. Holly tied down our canoe and gear while I dismantled the bug tent. The sun was just on the horizon and hovering under the clouds when the wind built to a deafening howl. An hour later the wind crashed into us, carrying a spray of light rain that whipped against our tent wall like some being trying to enter, the Dene hunters I imagined, throwing sticks and branches at the trespassers to run us off their hunting grounds.

I saw a flash of lightning and counted to ten Mississippi before I heard the following clap of thunder. Two miles away. Minutes later, another flash and this time I counted to five. Holly urged me to stay away from the tent walls and kneel on our foam mats. Another lightning strike illuminated the tent like fireworks. A second later, another strike, and we both twitched from whatever residual electricity passed through the ground and penetrated the insulation of our mats. Holly shouted, "Motherfucker." I laughed nervously.

The storm passed, and we took off our layers of clothing and slipped into our zipped-together sleeping bags. We held each other for warmth. I turned my back to Holly, and she spooned me with her hands on my stomach. We lay like that without talking, getting warm, feeling each other's warmth. I heard the claps of thunder, now in the distance, soothing like percussive music. Holly kissed the back of my neck, and I leaned into her lips.

She said, "I want to show you something. Think about your breathing, and I'll do the same."

Another meditation thing, and I did what she said. I focused on each breath and the movement of air in and out—rhythmic, steady. I felt Holly's breath behind me, matching mine, and we were in sync. We lay there breathing, concentrating on inhaling and exhaling together as one.

Holly said, "Hold my wrist and follow the pulse of my heart."

I felt it.

"Now let me hold yours. Now tap your finger on my wrist when you feel the pulse, and I'll do the same."

Strange, we were tapping at the same time and breathing at the same time, and we kept that rhythm. Holly said, "When people are in love, their hearts literally beat for each other. It's a proven fact."

What she said was as close to an expression of real love as I thought I'd ever heard in my life. She said it easily, the words just fell from her mouth like it was no big deal, but I was overcome with emotion.

We continued to feel each other's breath and pulse. Holly said, "The proximity up here amplifies a relationship. Ours is growing closer. You happy you came?"

I said, "Yes."

Before we slept, Holly said, "Tomorrow, we'll be at Thelon Canyon."

PART TWO

THE GLOAMING

12

Holly took another breath, then coughed again. I pulled her onto her side, and water dribbled from her mouth. I focused on each breath, ignoring the distant sound of the rapids that echoed off the canyon walls. The sun illuminated the side of her face until a stray cloud passed, and she slipped into its shadow.

I shouted, "Holly, Holly," but she didn't respond. I pulled her farther up onto the shore. Her Muck Boots were gone, and waves lapped at her socked feet. The cuts on the side of her face seeped blood that swirled across her cheek. She was breathing, rhythmically pushing air in and out, but her eyes were closed, and she didn't move. I just wanted Holly to look at me and respond, say my name, tell me she was okay.

I held her face and shook gently. "Holly, Holly." Her eyes remained closed and her body lay slack. I touched her hands. They shivered in mine, spasms that came in waves. I held them tightly, but they continued to shake. Her head started to shake, and spasms rippled through her chin that made her teeth chatter. I needed to get her warm and dry. I couldn't let her freeze to death.

I had no dry clothes, and no wood or matches to start a fire. My sleeping bag was wet. I could feel *my* body begin to shake with cold. The only option was to move, pump blood. I decided to climb back up the ravine to get the other P-pack with Holly's dry clothes and sleeping bag, and I needed to carry her with me. If I left her here, she would die from the cold.

The canyon walls loomed above me. I could maybe see the ledge where Holly had slipped and fell, where I left the other P-pack. It was so far away, and I couldn't be sure it was even the same one—the canyon stretched into the distance, and each ledge looked the same.

The ravine I came down was too steep to climb. To get back to the P-pack, I needed to move farther down the shoreline, farther away, to find another less steep ravine that I could climb. I pushed Holly's chest over my shoulder and then looped my arms around her thighs. I lifted and started walking. My wet boots sucked and sloshed as I stepped. Blood from the wound on my forehead pumped as I moved and drained into my right eye, nearly blinding me. I wiped away the blood and kept walking.

The next ravine was beyond an outcropping of stone, hundreds of yards in the distance. I walked past the outcropping and looked up. The ravine went deep into the walls of the canyon with a gradual incline. That I had a way up was a strange feeling of relief that I pushed from my mind. Nothing was over yet, and I tried to move faster.

My body had warmed by the time I started the climb, and I was sweating as I took each step that raised the bulk of us a few inches higher. Holly's weight pressed on my shoulder, my back, but I didn't dare stop and rest. If I set her down, I didn't think I could lift her again. I wouldn't lay her down until I reached the top.

I kept climbing. The rock was fragile sandstone that moved under my feet, and I tested each step. As I climbed, a dizziness overcame me. I felt weak, and on one incline, I did stumble. I fell forward and Holly's thighs jammed against the scrabble of rock. She made a sound, an *ugh* like a stab of pain. I shouted her name and stared into her face. I saw no recognition, no acknowledgment that I was here and with her. I knelt and pulled Holly back over my shoulder. I found solid footing and stepped up with the weight and kept climbing. I reached what I thought was the top of the canyon only to see another incline and maybe another false summit. I focused on each step, each push from the balls of my feet, each lift of the knee, and I could keep going as long as my legs held out. Finally, I reached the top and lay her down with her back against a chest-high granite rock. She was still shaking, her body shivering in waves.

My stomach convulsed and I vomited. A thin string of saliva hung from the edge of my mouth. Blood flowed from my jawline to my chin and then mixed with the saliva. I vomited again.

I unsheathed my knife, sliced the hem of my T-shirt, then ripped off a three-inch-wide strip from around my body. I wrapped it around my head twice to slow the bleeding and knotted the ends. I was sweating from the climb, hot. I lay down next to Holly, spooning her with my arms wrapped around her chest. Her shivering now had stopped. At first, I thought it a sign that she was getting better, warmer, but then her breathing slowed so that each breath came as a surprise. I held her wrist and felt a weak pulse, and now the thought that we were playing out the same embrace as the night before seemed cruelly ironic, a gesture of love turned to death. If I didn't get her warmed, she would die. I needed to shed her wet clothes, get her into a sleeping bag, or near a fire. I knelt and pulled Holly over my shoulder for the third time. I stood and continued walking.

The P-pack was where I'd dropped it, back where Holly had fallen. I unpacked her sleeping bag, unstuffed it, unzipped the seam, and laid it out like a blanket. I took off my clothes first, then undressed Holly. I unbuckled and unzipped the life vest and then took off her shirt and undershirt and lifted her onto the sleeping bag. I pulled off each wet sock, then yanked at her pants callously. Her eyes remained closed, her body slack. She barely breathed, taking one breath for every ten of mine. I lay down and covered us tightly with the bag. I held her and felt her cold body, and I continued to count every breath she took, every breath I took. I held her arms and touched her wrist. My fingers probed the edges of tendons, feeling for anything. Maybe a pulse but so faint. I counted my breaths and waited for hers. I counted to twenty before she took even one. My mind kept going back to the night before, our bodies in sync with our breaths and heartbeats pushing air and fluid together as though we were one being, alive. And now she was dying. I held her tight and close, my arms wrapped around her chest and stomach, my legs intertwined with hers, trying to leach the cold from her body. She continued to move air. My mind twisted through thoughts that only had meaning in their perversion—*If I loved Holly, then she would die.* If I didn't care, then she would live because that was how fate worked. Nothing I wanted or loved could ever be real—I wasn't fated to be chosen or lucky. It was so fucked-up, and I willed myself to stop thinking. I cleared my mind and tried to think of everything and nothing at the same time, like Holly had shown me in that field of flowers near the small lake. And I just let go.

I felt her rate of breathing gradually increase. Next came a convulsion of shaking muscles, and then I heard her teeth chatter. Her breathing quivered, but she moved air in increased cycles. I felt a stronger pulse. I held her until I could finally feel the warmth of our bodies together, until the shaking subsided and I could match my breathing and my pulse with hers. She was with me now, out of the canyon, out of the water, safe and warm. It felt like an accident with a happy ending, a story Holly could add to the journey of her life. But she wasn't conscious to tell me that, and I knew my optimism could just be an illusion.

13

I remembered the PLB, the personal locator beacon attached to Holly's life vest. The vest was with Holly's other clothes drying in the sun. I lifted it, turning it to where the beacon was clipped in a mesh pocket, but it was no longer there. I tried to remember if it was attached to the vest when I pulled her from the river. She always wore the PLB. I checked through the P-pack regardless and found nothing. We hadn't brought a satellite phone, and the PLB was the only way I could call for help. So stupid.

The blackflies were thick in the air, ever-present like the water and the sun. They bit at the sweat on my neck and face. The sting of bites had become little more than an itch that needed to be scratched. Then they descended on Holly. Her facial muscles twitched but she didn't move to protect herself.

Protecting Holly from the flies. That one thought, *protecting her*, stabbed me like the memory of stupid mistakes. I should have known, should have never let her get that close to the canyon's edge. I'd tried to say something that would get her attention, but nothing came from my mouth.

I pulled the tent from Holly's P-pack. I set it up on the hard surface of the sandstone shelf and found rocks to anchor the tie-downs of the tent canopy. I grabbed at the edges of the sleeping bag beneath her shoulders. I pulled her into the tent and then slapped at the bugs that had entered with us. Now she was warm, covered, and protected from the flies.

The reality of what was happening lay beside me. A near-fatal accident. Holly, comatose, needing hospitalization desperately, and me alone in this desolate wilderness. I needed help and had to find the PLB.

I backtracked to the riverbank, searching along the ground, around the rock where I'd laid Holly, and through the ravine. I searched along the river and then waded in to look beneath the surface for the bright yellow of its plastic casing. Would it be floating? I checked farther downstream until the walls of the canyon closed in and the next set of rapids blocked my path. Scattered pieces of my clothing—a T-shirt, a sock, a fleece sweatshirt—littered the shore. The bug tent with its fiberglass poles was gone. The fishing gear was gone. I collected the sleeping bag and the few clothes from the torn P-pack. I searched for the PLB upstream, wading through the whitewater and rocks. And there it was, just a flash of yellow sunk deep in the eddy of a rock.

I reached in up to my shoulder and pulled out the PLB. It looked like a child's toy walkie-talkie but with a red SOS button and a sophisticated screen with controls for moving and clicking a cursor. The screen was cracked and the display clouded. Back on shore I depressed the SOS button and watched for any movement on the screen. Nothing. I walked back to the top of the canyon with the wet sleeping bag and clothes that I'd recovered from the river.

The sun was sinking in the northwest, pushing to the end of the day. I unpacked my sleeping bag and draped it unzipped over the rocks to dry. The Leatherman multi-tool was in Holly's pack, and I used it to take off the back of the PLB and let the moisture evaporate. I crawled into the tent and lay next to Holly in my clothes that had dried on my body. The increasing cold drove me into a fetal position. I was covered, sheltered, and I didn't want to think about what to do next. Exhaustion overwhelmed me, and I knew I needed to close my eyes and sleep. I couldn't. Hours passed, and thoughts tumbled through my head, the same thoughts over and over—what I should have done, what went wrong, the fall, her near-drowning, anger at myself, anger at Holly for bringing me here. Then I thought of what I needed to do next. Holly could still wake up, we could still finish our trip, and I could wait here until she did. The best thing to do was just wait and hope.

She lay next to me breathing, but her eyes remained closed and her body remained lax and still. She'd endured a near-drowning, maybe leaving her brain starved for oxygen. I didn't know. She had scrapes on her face and possibly a head injury. I touched her hair and head, felt for a lump or a cut. At the base of her skull I touched a lump the size of a walnut. A concussion or a skull fracture. She could still wake up. If the PLB dried out and powered on, I could call for help.

SLEEP NEVER CAME. I stepped out from the tent just as the sun crested the horizon. The sky was clear and the wind still. I could hear the rapids just beyond the canyon ledge. Holly's phone lay where she had fallen. I could see its polished screen reflecting the sun's glare. I stepped toward the canyon, crawling the last few feet to reach the phone, too scared to look down. In my mind, I could still see her standing at the edge, smiling at her smartphone. I hadn't called out to warn her. She fell. I could still see her in the river reaching out for anything to stop her descent, then saw her in the hole, tumbling in the backflow of water.

I would need food. Hours of hiking were ahead of me to bring each food pack up from the beginning of the portage to where Holly lay in the tent. Two miles each way, and I couldn't leave Holly for long. I put on my still-wet boots. I took the first step and followed the cairns, the carefully laid piles of rock, like native guides leading me toward safety. But it wasn't safety I was walking toward, just the eighty pounds of food and supplies that had to be hauled up.

I started back up the canyon with the pack that held the lunch supplies and the first-aid kit. If Holly were awake, she'd be hungry, and I'd have the trail mix, cheese, meat, and crackers. Both water bottles were filled. The two-mile trip was a backbreaking journey with the eighty-pound pack—one foot methodically in front of the other, a pace that I could keep without stopping. My boots, still wet from the day before, made a sucking sound with each step. By the time I reached the tent, I could feel blisters starting to form.

The tent was still zippered shut. I opened it, hoping for movement or sound. But Holly lay where I'd left her, eyes closed, breathing. I found the tube of antibiotic ointment in the first aid kit and spread a light coating over Holly's cuts. They weren't deep and would heal on their own. I covered the cuts with gauze and tape.

The trip back down was weightless in comparison. I carried the second food pack but left the canoe. I pulled it farther up on shore and flipped it hull-side up. The cairns were my friends now, and they were all different. The one that marked the beginning had the note from Schuyler, "This 1,200-rod portage sucks ass." That cairn I dubbed The Messenger, but there were no other messages to deliver. Another cairn had been toppled and was now just a low mound of stones. I named this one Ruins. One had stick arms and a top rock like a head, and I called it Snowman. Each time I passed, I said their names, maybe just to hear my voice. The familiarity was reassuring, like I'd known the paths and trees of our land along the Platte.

I laid the second food pack next to the other. Holly was still unresponsive in the tent. I needed to decide about the canoe—to leave it or carry it up. I wanted to leave it because I was tired and exhausted. But it did no good at the start of the portage; I couldn't paddle back the way we'd come, which would've been upstream against the current. If Holly woke, I would need the canoe to continue downstream. And ultimately, I thought carrying it up was a luck thing, or fate, or optimism. Call it whatever. I knew that if I left it, then I didn't believe she'd wake up. I decided to make a last trip for the canoe.

I lifted the canoe onto my thighs, then flipped it onto my shoulders. I started walking. My legs felt rubbery and unsteady, and I walked carefully, locking each knee when I stepped like I imagined an amputee on two prosthetic legs. I tried to reach each cairn, each friend, before I stopped and rested. And every time I lay the canoe down, I had to find the strength to flip it back up and onto my shoulders. The last trip from the portage to Holly took hours.

When I reached the campsite, the sun was descending toward the horizon. I checked on Holly, who lay dead still in her sleeping bag. I pulled off my Muck Boots and spread out my socks to dry. The blisters on my heels were there, and I popped the bubble of skin with the tip of my knife.

What if she didn't wake up? What if she woke but couldn't continue portaging and paddling? And the other, darker thought hovered in the back of my mind like a specter overshadowing everything—*What if she died?* I was tired and couldn't think through every scenario. Or didn't want to think about them. I tried to cling to the idea that she'd wake up and continue the journey. Everything else was a turn in the road I didn't want to anticipate now. But that specter, her death, was like a headache that foretold a storm. I was scared.

The PLB could bring help immediately and get us both off this desolate river. The PLB was dry. I screwed the backplate onto the body of the device, then depressed the SOS button. The screen was unclouded but remained blank. The PLB was dead.

14

My sleeping bag was dry and I lay next to Holly, willing her to wake, look into my eyes, and say that she loves me. I touched her hair, thick like a horse's mane. I remembered that thought the first time I stroked it. Could she hear me? Was she just stuck inside her mind, as if trapped beneath a layer of ice, a frozen pane keeping her from the surface? Was she trying to call to me, reach for me? I needed to believe she was there, that she wanted to hear me speak. I'd planned to keep telling Holly more stories about my past. I told one now about the mother I never knew. Maybe she'd respond to the sound of my words.

I started, my voice echoing in the tent, loud enough, I hoped, to penetrate deep into her brain and subconscious, rattling the bars of her caged mind.

"Jake wanted me to think that my mother died in childbirth. I'd seen a birth certificate. I was born at the community hospital in Columbus. Her name was Ruby Harvey. Harvey was Jake's surname, and I assumed they were married. Jake said she died, but I never saw an obituary, a marker for her body, an urn of ashes, or a death certificate.

"He'd tell me about her. She looked like me, he said—dirty blond hair, squirrel cheeks, a broad face, big amber eyes. They'd met on the road, both part of a nomadic tribe of hippies following the Grateful Dead from gig to gig. Jake would see her at each concert sitting in a parking lot or along the road selling necklaces she threaded together herself, elaborate things that would cover a woman's chest like webbing. He told me she was talented, a real artist who had a following. After one show, Jake saw her hitchhiking with a sign that said simply, NEXT SHOW. He picked her up in his VW bus, and they traveled together after that. He helped her sell jewelry. Then she got pregnant. Jake said she loved being pregnant. She never had morning sickness, loved eating for two, loved the feel of her bulging stomach. Ruby let every hippie following the band rub her belly for good luck.

"Ruby was due around the time the Dead played Lincoln. The couple decided to end their traveling there and settle down. In a local newspaper Jake saw an advertisement for the land and unfinished house, and he had a small inheritance from a grandmother. He and Ruby drove up and bought the place. I was born a month later.

"I confronted Jake. I waited until late one night after he was stoned and almost ready for bed. I said that I couldn't find the obituary or any record of her death. I asked him honestly if she was still alive somewhere. He paused for a second. The lie was so much part of the fabric of our lives that I'm sure his instinct was to tell it again. But something stopped him, maybe the guilt of maintaining the lie, maybe because I was fourteen now and ready for the truth, or maybe because he was just stoned. What he said was, 'I don't know.'

"Then he told me what I believe is the truth. He said that the words Ruby used were, *I want to be open.* She wanted to be open to travel, open to new experiences, open to new people, and she wanted to continue to create and sell her art. She liked being pregnant, but when I was born, she didn't want to be a mother. Jake casually said that I didn't latch. Then she left, and he never saw her again.

"I asked him, 'What do you mean I didn't latch?'

"He said it again, 'You didn't latch.' He added that after I was born, I was taken away to be cleaned up and examined. An hour later a nurse came back with me while Ruby was in her hospital bed. Ruby held me and was overjoyed. She named me then, Lee. A joke at the time, Lee Harvey Oswald supposedly assassinated JFK. Ruby never believed he did it, said it was a conspiracy. She said I was a conspiracy. What that means I don't know, but I was the one stuck with the name. Then Ruby held me to her breast and my lips wouldn't latch. Jake said, 'You didn't latch on to her. I had to bottle feed you from the start.'

"So, Jake stuck me with that—I didn't latch on to my own mother, I rejected *her.* And he left me with the guilt of maybe being the one that pushed Ruby back on the road. After she left the hospital, Ruby never came back to the bunker. Jake said she just split, that he never saw her again. And I'm guessing that Jake's idea of raising a baby was to leave me in my alcove room and shove a bottle in my mouth every time I cried. A psychologist might say that because I never latched or attached, I have an attachment disorder. As a result, I'm emotionally abnormal.

"I asked Jake what her maiden name was. He said that they never married, and she never spoke about her family. She was just Ruby, and Jake wasn't sure Ruby was even her real given name.

"I asked him how I could find her.

"He said, 'I don't think you can. Think of her as an egg donor, like a sperm donor. Would you really want to know who that anonymous, disconnected person was?'

"When you told the story about Theo finding his sperm donor father, I thought of my mother. If I could, I would want to know her. But maybe like Theo, it might turn out to be a disappointment. She might not want to know *me*.

"At first, I was angry, like what kind of mother abandons her child? I had to imagine her selfish in a way that ignores everyone around her, a sociopath, or maybe just a drug addict. But one night I decided that I didn't need to be angry, that I could imagine her any way I wanted. What I imagined was an artist focused on her work and the life she intended to live, that she recognized in Jake his willingness and longing to raise and craft someone in his image. And that I'm okay and stronger because of it. I imagine that she still wants to know who I am, that I'm safe, but she knows it's no longer her place. My life is like the dead skin of a snake that she can no longer inhabit. She'd relinquished her motherhood rights. But I know she wishes me well."

Holly lay next to me. Her eyes opened but looked away unfocused. I said her name softly and then waited, watching Holly for any other sign that she heard me. Her eyes closed again. I watched for hours. Near sunrise I fell into a light sleep. I woke, hoping for any sign of consciousness, but there was none.

I could see the fork in the road, the eventuality that she might not wake up for days or at all, and there was little hope of a miraculous rescue. The realization sunk in, a dread that left an emptiness in my stomach, a hollowness. I forced myself to make a decision, one I wanted made for me. I remembered the pilot who had said that only ten groups paddled the Thelon each summer, but half of those came in from the Hanbury. At the confluence I stood a better chance of running into another group who could call for help. I decided to keep moving.

15

The canoe rested on my shoulders as I followed the cairns north to finish the portage and get back on the river to find help. I was guessing that the end of the portage was two miles away—five trips with the packs, gear, and Holly. The twenty miles of hiking would take more than ten hours—so much time. I needed to move faster.

The trail followed the sandstone bluff above the canyon. I kept walking without stopping. The trail descended into a marshy area filled with mosquitoes. My head netting wasn't zipped and my hands were clamped to the gunwales of the canoe, useless, as the bugs stabbed me over and over, hundreds of bites with mosquitoes plump from feeding on my blood. I knew I should've stopped to cover myself, but I didn't. I suffered the bites like a flagellant, my penance for being here, for following Holly, for letting her fall. I kept walking. The trail climbed and I had to carefully place my feet on each rock to keep the canoe from crashing down. Eventually, I was on top of the canyon again where cairns marked the trail. I acknowledged each one, but now they no longer seemed like friends, more like spectators of my penance, taunting me as I tried to finish the portage. Naysayers. I named one Knute, the pilot who'd warned us of the dangers, another was Jake the Snake, and one was the man who sold us the canoe. I called that cairn Royalex, or Royalass. I cursed each one, and the anger propelled me forward.

Finally, I came to one more descent to the shoreline, where another river from the east emptied into the Thelon. In the distance I saw the rippling whitewater of rapids that I'd need to navigate the next day. I set the canoe down, zipped up my head netting, and walked back. I pushed myself to move beyond the self-pity of penance.

Hours of walking, one hour each way, and now I was kicking each cairn as I went, toppling loose rocks that might've been stacked centuries ago. I didn't care. The straps of the food pack dug into my shoulders that were already sore from the day before. If I leaned over, the weight of the pack moved to my back and allowed some reprieve, but then my lower back started to ache from the stoop. My posture seesawed back and forth to distribute the pain. I ignored the sting from the popped blisters on my heels. I dropped the food pack next to the canoe and went back for the other.

The sun climbed in the sky and warmed the Barrens. I wanted to shed the thick bug shirt and face netting, but I chose to sweat rather than be eaten again by mosquitoes. I drank water and ate handfuls of trail mix to keep going.

I set down the second food pack and then went back for Holly and the P-pack. I pulled Holly from the tent by lifting her body up inches at a time. Her clothes had dried, and I slipped her pants onto her, inching them up each leg. I pushed Holly into a sitting position and pulled a T-shirt and the bug shirt over her head, then socks on her feet, but her boots were lost. I packed up the tent. I couldn't leave Holly out in the open at the end of the portage, and so needed to carry both her and the tent. I looped the shoulder strap of the tent bag over my head. It pulled at my neck like an anchor. I stood with Holly pressed over my shoulder and started walking. She made no sound.

Her body pressed on my back and legs, and within minutes I was sweating and thinking of how I could rest without laying her on the ground and having to lift her back up. I saw a knee-high boulder and stopped and sat with Holly still draped over my shoulder. I could feel her body and would have known it was her by the scent alone. I remembered once walking through the halls at college and smelling that same scent and knowing she'd walked through minutes before. The thought put a smile on my face that was erased a short time later when the toe of my boot caught on a stone. I nearly fell and dropped her. The stone was a reminder of where I was, what I was doing, like everything else in the Barrens that I could touch, taste, and smell.

I made it down the incline and again crossed the mosquito-infested meadow. I rested after climbing back up to the canyon bluff. I kept walking but slowed, stepping more carefully, like a pack mule. I stopped when tired at every boulder or ledge that allowed me to sit and rest. I passed a lone stunted black spruce, and it felt like the first time I'd really seen one. It was barely over my head but thick as a fifty-year-old tree. All its branches grew east away from the prevailing wind, and its trunk pressed against the west like a ship's bulwark. Part of me acknowledged the defiance of that tree in this inhospitable place, and part of me wanted to burn it down because it was one more reminder of the foolishness of being here. At the end of the portage I set up the tent and moved Holly back into shelter.

On my last trip, I carried Holly's P-pack. I'd been on the portage since the sun rose. Now the sun was moving down toward the horizon, and I knew I'd make it to the end before the sun set. I had a headache coming on, this one probably from dehydration, and I stopped to drink from my water bottle. I kept going, forcing my legs to move and propel me toward whatever ordeal came next. I kept hoping Holly would wake.

Our bug tent had been lost in the canyon. I sat outside surrounded by mosquitoes with my bug shirt closed over my head. I was too exhausted to cook. I forced myself to drink more water and eat more trail mix. I pulled off my socks and checked the blisters on my heels, which were now raw and bloody. I applied Band-Aids.

Holly's pack guitar was in a case outlined beneath the olive-green canvas of the P-pack. Inside the pack were her clothes, coats, and rain gear. I lifted out the guitar case with its top covered in stickers—Ely, Kawi, Surly Brewing, rainbow pride, Wall Drug, a peace sign, others. I opened the case and slid out the smooth lacquered instrument. I held it and touched the length of its neck. It was a piece of Holly like her hair or lips. I entered the tent with the instrument. She lay in her sleeping bag, her eyes closed as though just sleeping. I wanted to wake her with a sound she knew. I positioned my fingers on the frets and touched the strings. The shock of sound startled me. I looked at Holly whose eyes remained closed, her face locked in an expression like some embalmed corpse. But she continued to take one widely spaced breath after another.

The portage trailed behind me now. Tomorrow I'd have to navigate the rapids.

16

The mosquito bites had raised welts on my face like boiling acne. The wrapped cloth around my forehead was crusty with dried blood, and I didn't dare untie it to feel for the depth of the cut that would require attention before infection set in. I knew I needed more sleep, to eat food and drink water. And how long could Holly last with neither food or water? How long could she stay in her comatose state? I knew about hunger and thirst. A body could live without food for weeks, feeding off its stored fat and muscle. But the lack of water would kill Holly way before that, maybe in days. Her bodily functions would just shut down one by one.

I couldn't sleep. My anxiety plagued me like an itchy blanket as I wormed in my sleeping bag for hours.

In the morning I was crouched in the tent, going over the maps I'd found in Holly's pack. Of the six, we'd just crossed over onto the third. Tight bands of rising elevation marked the Thelon Canyon, and I traced the portage to where we were now. The river from the east was the Clark, and I wasn't far from the confluence of the Hanbury and Thelon rivers. At the confluence I hoped to find help. I packed up.

I laid Holly in the bow of the canoe, her feet against the front deck, her back and head resting against the P-pack. I pushed off from the shore and entered the last whitewater of the Canyon. I saw the path to take, and followed the deep water between rocks. It was an easy set that Holly would not have bothered to scout. My only concern was keeping the canoe straight and off the rocks without a bow paddler's strokes.

I hit the first drop at an angle, and the foot-high standing wave below turned the canoe sideways. I felt the wave pulling the gunnel down, and I saw Holly's body slide to the low side. I realized just then that if I dumped, she'd go into the river, and even with her life vest, she'd drift from the canoe and drown. I was scared that I'd kill her, horrified that I had been so stupid to not think through every possibility. I dug in and paddled harder and quicker to get the bow back around. Finally, it turned, and I muscled the canoe past the wave and saw the next drop farther on. I looked for any slack water or eddy to pull over and stop but found none—no way to avoid running the rest of the rapids. I just needed to do it, and willed myself to not fuck up. I back-paddled and slowed my descent, buying time to make sure the canoe was pointed downriver before hitting the drop. I hit it straight on and the bow pushed through like a sharp plow through garden soil.

The set emptied into a wide stretch of river, and I pulled off, too wired and scared to keep going. I could've lost Holly if the canoe had dumped. She would've drowned and I'd be alone wishing I were dead, too. I sat on the shore and calmed myself. Days earlier I would have been exhilarated, a whitewater junkie. Now I was just frightened. And I knew I couldn't portage every set of rapids—I needed to keep moving. I tied a length of rope, a tether, from Holly's waist to the front thwart. If I did dump, then Holly wouldn't drift far from the canoe.

I got back on the river and started paddling, and now I stopped to scout every set no matter how easy or obvious. I visualized each rock and turn in the rapids, looking for obstacles that might swamp the canoe. I took my time, back-paddled, and lined up the bow before following my route. I learned another thing—if I knelt closer to the center of the canoe, the changed fulcrum of my paddle strokes would compensate for the lack of a bow paddler.

In the late afternoon I canoed past a set of rapids cascading into the Thelon from the west, the Hanbury River. I camped a mile farther down at the point of a sandbar island, a place where anyone who passed the confluence would spot my tent.

After I had Holly settled in her sleeping bag, I walked the shoreline looking for driftwood. I searched for an hour and found none. Then I came across a flat, open field where I saw ragged holes from pulled-up tent stakes. Nearby, beneath the camouflage of caribou moss, I uncovered a wooden cooking spoon that had been forgotten or lost. Along the thick hand-carved handle was an inscription that said, "The life of a Voyager." I figured the words were meant to be nostalgic or inspiring. To me, now, they meant only hardship. At the end of the spoon, still-soft food encrusted the tip—a sign that others were near.

17

From my knees I looked down into a pool of water balanced above the tundra permafrost. The first length of cloth wrapping uncoiled from my head easily, the second length stopped at the gash. The reflection splintered when my hand dipped into the water and dampened the cloth to soften the caked blood. It took time, the water working its way into cotton and dead cells, releasing interlocked bonds. The cloth came away in fits and starts and tugs of pain. The pooled water settled and I could see the gash to the side of my face that was ragged and bone-deep. The swelling from mosquito bites had diminished to pox-like scabs, and I looked like some comic book zombie. Blackflies swarmed to the blood and moisture. I brushed them away from the wound but let them feed freely from the back of my neck. I dipped the clean end of the cloth in the water and worked it into the wound to scrape out sand and dirt. Blood started to flow again. From Jake I'd learned the healing effect of a simple sugar wrap, a natural preservative that kills bacteria. We'd used it on animals and ourselves, and I needed to save the finger-length tube of antibiotic ointment for Holly. By my side was a fresh length of cloth and a cup partially filled with sugar. I dumped the sugar on the cloth and then pulled it against my wound. I wrapped it twice and knotted the ends.

In the tent I heard the whitewater that tried to drown out my hamster wheel of thoughts. I wanted to talk to Holly, wanted her to wake up and take control of this fucking trip. She was next to me with her eyes closed. I looked toward her and told a story, one she knew. I was hoping to somehow break through whatever was clouding her brain. I needed her to wake the fuck up.

"You were anyone's vision of a beautiful woman—long brown hair, thin, smaller breasts, an intelligent face. Your eyes were intense like you were staring at some speck of food on my lip, and I think you were just looking for any nuance that might add to what I was saying. I was attracted to you at the coffee shop right off. When you sat down and started talking to me, I wanted to touch your hand.

"You asked if we could exchange phone numbers, and I said, 'Yes.' You said to give you my phone number, that you'd call it and send me yours. I told you my number but that it was the number in my dorm, the number to a public phone down the hall that only I ever used. I told you I didn't own a cell phone or smartphone, and you said, 'Cool.' You said you were addicted to the thing but thought it kept you from looking around, seeing the world. You said, 'Like blinders on a horse.' I told you that I didn't know the difference, that I'd never owned a cell phone, and that I'd never worn horse blinders. You thought that was funny, and then you told me that we should do something, maybe go to an art opening later in the week. I said, 'Okay.'

"Two days later we met at a restaurant in College Hill. It was after six on a Friday and we both ordered pints of beer and sat at a small table overlooking the street. We did the usual get-to-know-you patter—where are you from, how did you get here. We were both from the Midwest, so I didn't have to explain where Nebraska was and feel like some freak from the Great Plains. You liked that I raised animals and worked a garden for food. I could tell you liked that I was self-sufficient, that I wasn't scared to work and get dirty, and maybe then you thought I was someone you could take to the Barrens. It was clear that you came from the other, better, side of the tracks. You used your phone to get us an Uber to the show. We drove to a boxing gym in Lower South. In Nebraska, we'd call the building a pole barn—one story, cheap steel siding, no windows, an oversized garage door. Women stood smoking in small groups outside the entrance.

"Inside, the gym was packed with mostly women. You took my hand and pulled me through the crowd. Along one side hung a row of long cylindrical punching bags dangling from chains. A line of people stood between the bags and the wall looking at gallery photos. In back was a raised boxing ring surrounded by onlookers. In the ring, above the heads of the crowd, I could see two naked women, and I thought that was really strange. We made it to a bar of sorts, two women identically dressed in jeans and sleeveless T-shirts, both with their heads shaved, serving cans of beer from an iced trough. I bought us two cans and we moved on. You seemed to know everyone, and I was introduced as your friend Lee. It was loud, with sound coming from the boxing ring, muffled music, endless talking. It smelled horrible—a mix of sweat, leather, perfume, and cigarettes.

"We moved near the boxing ring, where the two naked women were dancing out a weird push-and-pull pantomime. Each had their ankles and wrists tied with rope that strung back to pulleys under the mat. The one woman's wrists and ankles were attached to the other's so that if one moved a hand forward, the other had to move her hand back, and they moved around the ring, reaching and pulling, each hand or foot coming close to the other's but not allowed to touch. Of course, the symbolism wasn't lost on either of us. You thought it was cool and said, 'Sometimes we can't be ourselves.' I was cynical and just said, 'I wonder what they do at the end of round one—maybe give it a rest.' Cynical. And to myself, I said, *Shut the fuck up.* We kept moving.

"Behind the line of punching bags and against the wall were a series of photos. I could see that the idea was to view each with the punching bags behind you, pushing you up close and personal, and we stood in line to move through the gauntlet of bags. The first photos were blurry with color, like cheap snapshots, and I couldn't make out the image. As we moved through, the photos became more and more in focus until I knew what I was looking at. I realized that my face was being pushed into images of a vagina. With each photo the camera angle moved back and more of the woman's torso was exposed, then another woman moved into the frame with her face next to the vagina, then her tongue close and touching. The woman had your thin face, your long nose, and I realized the woman in the photo was you. I was stunned and looked up to you beside me. You just looked back and smiled. You said, 'My friend asked me to pose for her project.' Then you shrugged your shoulders, like, *what are you gonna do*? I just laughed.

"At the end of the match the ring was cleared of the rope and pulley contraption, the music turned up, and the boxing ring filled with dancing women. You were a crazy dancer, moving fluidly like oil in water. I was all jerky movements in my jeans and flannel shirt. My long dirty-blond hair swirled all moppy around my head. My androgynous look—jeans, boots, and flannel—fit right in, but I doubted my luck to be with such a beautiful woman. I liked you—I really liked you. We kissed."

My story was finished. I looked at Holly. I said, "I love you." It was the first time I'd said those words, and now I believed them and knew I would say the words over and over when she woke.

Her eyes opened. Her head turned slightly, and her eyes focused on mine. She looked at me as though she'd listened to the story. I said her name, "Holly, Holly."

Her eyes closed.

I knelt above and shook her shoulders. I said her name louder, "*Holly*."

Her eyes remained closed. Her mouth tightened into a grimace of pain. I stopped shaking but looked into her face, waiting for her eyes to open again and recognize me. I looked for any sign that Holly was still with me, any hope that she would recover, that we'd continue the journey that now felt like it had slipped between my fingers and left me with nothing but pain. I wanted Holly to tell me more stories, more imagined stories of us. I wanted to continue telling my story. And I wanted to tell her again that I loved her.

18

I saw a jetliner thirty thousand feet above me at the head of a contrail streaking the sky, maybe a flight from Seattle to Amsterdam taking the fastest route with passengers lying back, drinking wine, popping Ambien to dream their way to Europe.

Think. Maybe ten groups canoed the Thelon each summer. Were they ahead of me? Behind? Could I just stay at the confluence of the two rivers and get discovered? Could I be 100 percent certain? No, I needed to keep moving. I might catch a group, I might get found, I might have to paddle the entirety of the fucking Thelon. I needed Holly to come out of her coma, or I needed to run into another group on the river with a PLB or satellite phone. If not, I feared she would surely die.

I laid the maps out on the sand beach, holding down the edges with rocks. The river was lined up so that the five maps remaining showed its progression from where I was now all the way to Baker Lake, a meandering route north and east. Other rivers emptied into the Thelon, but the Thelon itself ran three hundred or more miles toward its inevitable destination. All I needed to do was keep the bow of the canoe pointed downriver, and worry about the big lakes of Beverly and Aberdeen when I got there—if I got there. The current map, 65M Clark River, would take me another hundred miles, four or five days, and then I'd be only halfway.

I set Holly in the bow of the canoe with her bug shirt zipped over her head. I stepped in with one foot on the keel line, pushing off with the other.

The river braided through channels in the sand. I stayed to what I thought was the deep water and main channel. Gradually, the sand, crushed rock, and lichen-covered granite of the Barrens gave way to taller black spruce and stands of birch. I knew from the map that I was moving into the Oasis. Holly had talked about this stretch of the river, a wooded sanctuary filled with wildlife like musk oxen, moose, bear, and wolves. And I did pass two musk ox grazing on a slope of green tundra shrubs. They were like the farm-raised buffalo back in Nebraska but smaller and shaggier, with horns that swooped down beside their massive heads and curled into hooks. Both looked up to see me on the river. They sluggishly moved farther away.

I paddled from the stern, every stroke a J-stroke to keep the canoe going straight without the counterstroke of a bow paddler. I favored my left side but switched to lessen the searing pain in my hands. Blisters ran along both palms and up two middle fingers where the bulge of fat and muscle met the plastic of the paddle handle.

I pulled off at a place on the map labeled Warden's Grove. Beneath the high-water mark of the riverbank was a fire ring of rocks that would be washed away by the spring floods. The charred remains of driftwood were cold but brittle and fresh. Someone had been here recently, maybe within days. At the top of the riverbank I found a path through the spruce. I left the canoe on the shore with Holly still in the bow and followed the path. Around a corner I saw the grass-covered roof of a cabin, then the log walls. I moved quicker, almost running. I hoped someone lived there who had a radio or some way to contact the outside world. I could get Holly to a doctor who would bring her back. But then I saw the doorway without a door and windows with broken glass. The remnants of a sheet-metal chimney lay prone on the roof, and in a nearby field of wintergreen shrubs sat the rusting stove. I ducked through the low doorway and found a shattered half of a whiskey bottle that was tinted amber, irregular, and hand-blown—no sign that anyone had lived here for decades.

I SET UP camp at the Grove and moved Holly into the tent. I ate trail mix, drank water, and changed the sugar wrap on my head.

Holly lay in her sleeping bag with her head resting on my bundled sweatshirt. Her eyes were closed, her mouth open, and her lungs slowly moved air in and out. I sat beside her with water and a length of cloth. Her lips were dry and cracked—she needed water. I moistened the cloth and touched it to her lips, then squeezed drops into her mouth. I wanted to see her tongue move to swallow, but nothing. I squeezed a few more drops. The water slipped down into her throat until she reflexively choked and coughed. I pulled her body toward me so that the drops could drain to the floor of the tent, so that she could spill the water from her airways. She coughed twice and stopped. I lay her back with her head resting again on the sweatshirt. I touched her hair and brushed strands away from her face. I leaned down to kiss her cheek. I hoped she'd wake up, look at me, and say something. Nothing.

I told her a story about the time before we met, a painful story I would've never revealed to her or anyone. If she heard me and remembered, then so be it.

"When I came to Brown, I acted like a deer caught in the headlights, like that deer I'd shot on the side of the road. I looked and talked differently, and I felt like some kid from another country, like I didn't know the language or the culture—the ways to interact. I wanted to meet someone, but I didn't know how, and I certainly didn't know about Tinder or have a smartphone to use it. Then in the dining hall I had no one to sit with, and I was petrified to make friends. I'd sit in this one room designated for those who needed quiet time to study—or for rejects like me who needed to sit alone. Then one day this woman sat down, maybe just like you had, and started talking, I guess coming on to me. I was flattered. I'd seen her before, looking my way in calculus class.

"Her name was Corinna. I thought she looked pretty, with blond hair pumped up in a pompadour and a silver ring through her nose like a bull back home. It was smaller, of course, and turned out to be fake and not through her septum, but at the time I thought it attractive and a bit exotic. I was intimidated. She asked about me and I told her lies that made me look normal, adult. I was still from Columbus, but my father was a lawyer, a prosecutor, and my mother was a schoolteacher. I based the lie on people I knew so that the story wouldn't seem made-up or contrived. We started dating. I got clingy.

"Corinna was two years older and lived off campus, but unlike your apartment, hers was a dump—a studio with a couch that folded out into a bed, a bathroom with moldy tiles, dirty dishes always in the sink. But at least it wasn't my dorm room triple designed to be a double. She was kind at first, letting me stay at her place whenever I wanted, and she gave me advice on classes, professors to know, and ones to avoid. Corinna definitely took the lead in sex and told me what to do and how to do it. I was inexperienced. I'd had only one other fucked-up encounter, and I wanted the touch of another woman. I did what she said, and for a time I enjoyed it.

"Then things got weird. A month into the relationship Corinna wanted me to spend every night at her apartment. She said over and over that she loved me and pushed me to say the same, though I hardly knew what that meant. One time I just didn't go back there, and she called my dorm and started yelling, accusing me of sleeping with someone else. The yelling turned to crying and then pleading. I said that I'd come to her place, and by the time I got there, she'd calmed down and was all nice like nothing had happened. And I stayed at her place after that. I guess I didn't want to upset her again. And my dorm situation did suck.

"Then the sex got weird, too. It had always been, *do this, do that*, but now it was less of a please tone and more like the way Jake would command me—*DO this, DO that*. She was older, dominant, and I did what she asked. Then one time I was on my stomach and Corinna was above, on top. I felt something other than her fingers or tongue go into my vagina, and I said to her, 'What are you doing?' She just said, 'Hold still,' and she kept doing it like I was supposed to like it or something, but I didn't. I lay there until she finished. Afterward, I could see it was a longneck beer bottle, one of the Rolling Rocks she'd been drinking. She said nothing and I said nothing. I should have said something, but I didn't.

"It got worse. She'd want to know my schedule and when I'd be home. She wanted me to do all my homework at her apartment and eat my meals there too. I fucking cooked and cleaned for her like I'd done for Jake in the bunker. I tried to avoid sex, but when she wanted it, she was demanding, and I felt I had to comply. And she did more things without asking, then slapping and using names like *bitch* and *slut*. How that intersected with *I love you* was beyond my comprehension. I was already into Google by then and knew I was deep into an abusive relationship. The advice online was simple—leave.

"One night I built up the courage to just say stop, that I was uncomfortable. Corinna said, 'Shut the fuck up.' And that was it, just those four words that I'd heard from Jake my entire life. I snapped out of it and decided to leave that night. We fought, and she pleaded with me to stay. She tried to grab and hold me, but I must've outweighed her by fifty pounds. I just pushed through her and left. But it didn't end there. She called that night and the next day and again that night. Crying, yelling, pleading, then finally saying that she'd kill herself if I didn't come back.

"So, Holly, what do you do in that situation? Relent to appease her, stop her? Risk that it's just a bluff? It was a fucked-up catch-22. I searched Google again, where I found a suggestion that I call someone at Counseling and Psychological Services on campus. The person I spoke with took my call seriously and said they'd call Corinna and have the police do a wellness check. Fine, I was off the hook.

"Corinna stopped calling me, and when we passed in the halls or in class, she treated me like a non-person. That was okay with me.

"When I met you, I didn't lie about my life in Nebraska or my relationship with Corinna, but I didn't talk much about it either—I guess I told half-truths, real facts with omissions. I thought you understood my reluctance and knew that I'd talk about everything in my own time, at my own pace, maybe on this trip. And you were kind to me, and we moved into sex slowly over the course of weeks, learning to like each other first. And then we did have sex, moving to discover each other's body and pleasure over time. Talking and asking. I thought I'd found normal.

"I remember something you said to me, 'When it first feels right and then it's wrong, you think wrong is right.' You said it about something you were doing in class, but it struck me as something you'd say about Corinna—or Jake—if you knew them."

I WOKE THE next morning to the sound of another jetliner pushing its way across the sky. I tried to think of what our tent looked like from thirty thousand feet. At that height I imagined being able to see the curvature of the earth, clouds below like white puffs of mold on cheese, the curvy Thelon like a loose thread on camo clothing. They wouldn't see the tent, or plumes of smoke if I put a match to the old trapper cabin, hell, they'd barely notice a nuclear explosion. The passing jetliner crossed the sky, leaving behind a deadness of sound.

I set fire to the trapper cabin anyway. The wood was rotting and dry. I started the fire in one corner with kindling stripped from the logs. I stood inside the cabin and watched as the flames moved up the two walls and then into the roof. I stepped outside and looked on from a distance. The heated roof of dirt and grasses sent up billows of smoke, and I hoped someone somewhere could see the fire. I hoped it spread to the tundra and became a wildfire that firefighters couldn't ignore. The trapper cabin was engulfed in flames and the nearby brush caught fire, but the surrounding bog of tundra was everywhere and too wet to burn. The fire diminished within hours and smoldered for the rest of the day. I didn't see or hear another plane.

I ate a meal of pasta cooked over the embers and then went back into the tent and tried to sleep. Holly lay in her sleeping bag, breathing, her eyes closed. I eventually slept.

I woke up groggy and half-conscious. I heard another jetliner cross the sky, too late and too high to see any lingering smoke. My mind drifted as I lay in the sleeping bag. I thought of Holly, and I tried to remember when it was that I knew I loved her. Was it an epiphany? Did she say one thing or do one thing that switched on the light? Some things seemed trite but with an element of truth. Our bodies fit together—Holly was thinner and taller and covered mine like a candy wrapper. We learned to be comfortable in our silences—I could study quietly across from her in the library, and we could sit in a coffee shop and just be in our own thoughts. Maybe the sex was just that good. I thought it was all those things, the culmination of touches, talking, sex, silence, and times apart. Over time, I gradually learned that I loved her. I learned to want Holly without exceptions, with no rules. I loved that she was pushing me to be a different person—more open, confident, maybe calmer, and able to see life in different ways. I could feel the change and I was still changing. I wished I had told her sooner.

I reached over to touch Holly, her hair and skin. I touched her with my lips. But what I felt was cold.

The silence left behind by the jetliner was absolute.

19

"I was eight years old when Jake made me play the kick-the-can game, or as he put it, blow-up-the-can. I later called it the alone game. The whole state forest between the bunker and the river was our playground. A path divided the forest into my side and his. About five hundred yards into each side were two old Hills Brothers coffee cans standing upside down with a fuse sticking out the top. Beneath each can was an M-80, really a quarter stick of dynamite. The rules were simple. The game started at sunset when both of us had to be at our can. The first to blow up the other's can won. And if either was tagged in the other's territory, they lost.

"We played that first game in July when the forest was thick with leafed-out brush and deep grasses, the sky clear, and the moon full or near full. That first night I sat guarding my can, making sure Jake couldn't blow it up, or if he got close, I could tag him. I waited for hours. I watched the moon cross the sky and then disappear. The feeling of being alone in the forest in the dark of night was overwhelming. It wasn't the fright of animals. I'd been with Jake in the night stalking game. I knew the sounds of the night, and I'd been taught how to guide myself home by the moon or the stars—Polaris was north, and the Big Dipper always pointed toward Polaris. On pitch-black nights we could follow the glow from the town's streetlights. But on that first night of the can game I was in the forest alone and without Jake. The feeling of aloneness magnified the emptiness left by friends I never had, the mother I never had. It made me scared that I'd lose Jake, and I started to believe that he'd already left. I fell asleep crying. I was startled awake when Jake lit the fuse and the can exploded into the air like a rocket.

"We played again in August. I was scared to be left alone at my can as the sun went down, and I knew that the loneliness would set in and overwhelm me. What I chose to do instead was move. His can was east of the dividing path and in a clearing I knew well. I walked to the path, then got my bearings. I moved into his territory, stepping only on grasses to muffle my footsteps, pushing aside branches with the tips of my fingers. Jake was waiting for me. He'd seen me or heard me or just knew where I'd go. He came running and tagged me before I made it a hundred yards from the path. We didn't play again until the following year.

"The blow-up-the-can game was simple in its rules—to win, blow up the other's can or tag them in your territory. What I quickly understood was that if no one leaves the safety of their can, if no one leaves their can unguarded, then no one can win. And the first person to leave their can unguarded to blow up the other's, usually loses. So, the games that second year were about who could wait the longest. But then there was the issue of food, water, and sleep.

"That first game in July I stayed by my can throughout the night. I was a year older, nine, and I thought myself more confident in my ability to wait and stalk. I didn't feel as alone in the forest, and I spent the night listening for any sound of Jake's movements. I was still alert in the morning when the sun rose. I sucked the dew off leaves. I figured Jake wouldn't make any movement until nightfall, so I didn't either. I slept for part of the day and nothing happened. By that night I was hungry and thirsty. I moved from my can. I stayed on my side of the path but next to it so that I could hear or see Jake as he tried to move into my territory. Clouds came in and it rained. My thirst was quenched, but I couldn't hear or see a thing. I should have moved back to my can to protect it, but by the time that realization came, I heard the explosion and saw the rocket tail of sparks. Jake had won again.

"In early August of that year, Jake came into my room and said to get my things together, that we were playing the can game again that night. I was already tired from working in the garden and we'd spent hours on the highway selling produce off the back of the truck. I wasn't in the mood and I just said, 'I don't want to, Jake, what's the point?'

"He said, 'People see a queue of others, and they just step behind the last person in line. People are lemmings that will eventually follow each other off the edge of a cliff. You need to know how to be alone; you need to be able to think for yourself. Nothing can bring you independence and assurance but yourself.'

"I said, 'If I win this *alone* game, can I be done?'

"He said, 'Yes.'

"I dressed that night in clothes I used for hunting—all browns and forest greens. I wore a black watch cap low over my forehead. By sunset I was at my can. I was still there the next morning.

In daylight I dug a hole with my hands that filled with water, and I filtered out the mud by depressing my hat into the hole. I drank but didn't eat. I slept lightly at midday and spent the next night guarding my can. I didn't move until the third night. Then I moved slowly and soundlessly toward the path. When I was close, I dropped to the ground and crawled inch by inch, pausing to listen for any sound of Jake. I guessed that he was doing the same. I crossed into his territory and kept crawling. At times I waited for a freight train screaming through Columbus to cover the sound of my advance.

"Then I saw him, just movement along the ground like waves on a lake, almost imperceptible. He was still on his side of the path but moving toward mine. I lay as close to the ground as I could, slowing my breathing. I froze and waited for Jake to pass. Then I felt something crawl into my pant leg. I thought it might be a spider or a salamander, but then it felt larger, a snake. I knew it could be a poisonous copperhead, but most likely just a garter. I couldn't see it or bend over to pull it out. I waited until the next freight train came through and then I moved. I reached down and yanked the snake out by its tail, then crouched into a quick run. The train passed and I lay flat again, listening for Jake. I heard nothing. I figured he was still crawling toward the path. Then I took a gamble. I grabbed the lighter in my pants pocket, stood up, and ran. I made it to the edge of his clearing and could see the moonlight reflecting off the metal can. Jake was running my way when I struck the flint of the lighter. The fuse was lit by the time he reached me. We both stepped back and watched the can explode into the air.

"I looked at him then. I was tired and I was mad. I said, 'Did you really need to teach me how to be alone?'

"He said that I would thank him later. I would know in the future that what he did for me was more than just useful, that it was crucial.

"I was done with the alone game then. I'd never wanted to be left alone. And now you left me alone."

20

Holly lay next to me, her face exposed to the fouled air inside the tent that she no longer breathed. I lay next to her for hours in a dreamlike state, not wanting to face the reality of what to do next. Sometimes I looked at her and expected her to take a breath, just as I'd expected her to wake from her comatose state. I left the tent once to relieve myself near the river. The blackflies swarmed to my face and followed me back into the tent. The smell of her evacuated body was now overwhelming, forcing me to acknowledge what was happening. The flies landed on Holly's face, covering it like ants on discarded fruit. I watched the flies, hoping Holly would lift her hand to shoo them away. Hope was fading. The reality of her death set in like anger. You left me alone.

I knelt over Holly and brushed away the flies, my fingertips touching her skin. Her face was ghost white. Her eyes were partially open now, the green of her irises clouded and bluish. Her mouth remained open, frozen from when she took the last breath that I never heard. I lifted her chin to close her mouth. The muscles of her jaw had stiffened, and her mouth sprung back so that

I could see her teeth, her tongue. I brushed away the flies again. I knew this would be how I'd picture her face for some time, the image of her dead eyes and open mouth overriding past images of her smiling or laughing. I pulled the edges of the sleeping bag up over her head and pulled the drawstring. I tied two slipless knots to close it airtight. I lay next to her for hours as the gauzy aura of the sun moved across the roof of the tent. I fell asleep crying.

The dream was vivid. I was holding Holly in my arms, but hers hung slack. Her eyes were open, her mouth was open, and I waited for her to speak. I wanted her to hold me in response. I wanted her to say that she loved me because I'd just told her that I loved her. We were on the bridge over the Providence River, and below, the water was pushed into whitecaps from the cold wind. I didn't want to say more because I didn't want to lead her on. She had to say, 'I love you,' on her own. Her mouth was open but not moving, and her eyes were lifeless. I knew something was wrong. Then we were on the cliff overlooking the gorge of the Thelon. The ground gave way, and we were falling together toward the water and I saw the rocks beneath the surface move toward us and I knew we were going to hit the rocks and water. We were going to crash against the rocks—we were going to drown.

I woke up sweating. It was still light outside, the sun just below the horizon, the gloaming. I wanted to cry again, lose myself in that catharsis, the self-pity of that release. I wanted to cry for Holly who lay next to me, lifeless. But nothing happened; the tears I wanted wouldn't come.

Holly was dead, a nightmare I couldn't wake from. I was alone on the Barrens, on a river that flowed only one direction. I thought of how easy it would be to lay next to Holly day after day and eventually die—no more pondering how I was going to get

down the river and back to civilization and her family, no understanding of how the tragedy would play out in the weeks, months,
and years ahead. Just lay down and be done. But as I had those
thoughts, I pushed up to my knees and crawled from the tent. I
stepped out into the dim light of the morning. I pulled on my
Muck Boots and moved to pack up and get back onto the river. I
continued to put one step in front of the other. It was all habit, an
ant trail that led to food, then shelter, then some unknown eventuality, and it was not my place to figure out why or judge why
not. Keep moving and face whatever came next. It would happen
and I could just let it happen.

I inched Holly slowly from the tent and down to the canoe.
Her body in the sleeping bag was heavy and awkward in its post-
mortem rigidity. I tipped the edge of the canoe toward her and
propped up the hull with rocks. I slid Holly into the bow and,
after packing up, pushed off and onto the river.

21

I paddled through the Thelon Oasis. Taller spruce and birch lined the river. I saw signs of wildlife in the tracks left at the edge of the water, and then I passed three grazing musk ox who looked up when they heard the sound of my dipping paddle. One looked to be a bull, the others a cow and a calf. The bull led the two away from the river and the stranger gliding past. The calf was hornless and hadn't grown the shaggy dark-brown coat needed for winter. The fur of its legs was dusty white from its knees down, like a child's rain boots. It felt strange that the living were still around me—the musk ox with their offspring, the flies swarming to the warmth and blood of my body, animals descending to the Thelon to drink.

My hands stung with the pain of raw and broken blisters, and each time I switched sides, I saw smears of blood on the handle and shaft. What had Holly said? *You'll just have to tough it out.* For long stretches along the river, I felt numb—the pain was outside my body. I didn't feel anything. I wanted to grieve, but I didn't know how.

The afternoon sun was hot, and I stripped to a long-sleeved T-shirt. I guessed the temperature was near seventy degrees. Before a turn in the river I smelled a dead trout before I saw it. I paddled on the right side of the canoe, moving its bow to follow the curving shore. In the distance it was there, a trout surrounded by a congress of ravens feasting on its rotting flesh. The sight startled me out of the rhythmic movement of paddling. Holly's body would begin to rot, and I knew I couldn't stay on the river in this weather, in this heat. I needed to keep her body cold.

I stopped at a cairn on the northwest side of the river where it expanded into a cove out of the main current. I pulled the canoe's bow up onto a beach of rocks and then unloaded the packs. I dug out the nylon rope we'd packed. I cut three lengths and tied each end to one of six rocks the size of softballs. I used the crown knot Jake had taught me, four knots to enfold each rock in netting. I looped the weights around my neck, then lifted Holly from the canoe and set her into a foot of icy water. The rigor mortis was beginning to disappear from Holly's body, and now I lifted and carried her in my arms with more ease. I laid each length of rope over her chest and legs to keep her submerged. I tethered a rope from her midsection to a tree to make sure the current didn't pull her free. Until the weather changed, I would need to paddle in the cooler temperatures of the night and keep Holly's body chilled in the waters of the Thelon during the day.

22

I moved through the gloaming. I could see only the contours of the river, the darker lineation of ripples. The northern landscape was a silhouette against the glow of light from beneath the horizon. My eyes were drawn to the light, and the southern landscape was all but forgotten. I felt the temperature drop into the forties and I pulled out my fleece sweatshirt and wore it over the bug shirt. A strong wind kept the mosquitoes and blackflies off me, so I paddled without head netting. The sky was clear but with enough dim light to blot out the stars. The half-moon was translucent, a ghost. I kept paddling. The tiredness I felt was overwhelming, past paranoid to a numbness that made me forget everything. I felt an appetite and a thirst like the recollection of sun. I knew I'd drink and eat, but not enough, and not now.

A gust of wind caught my bow and turned the canoe like the hands of a clock. For a moment I felt disoriented, and then a strange reflection of light on the sandy shore appeared like a mirage as a turn in the river. I followed the mirage of water and paddled up onto the beach, the bow skidding to a stop. I shook my head at the stupidity. I pushed off and kept going.

Later, toward sunrise, I heard the rush of whitewater on a stretch of the river where no rapids were marked. Was I lost? Was it possible that I'd taken a fork in the river that sent me up or down another course? The sound was deafening, and before a bend in the river I pulled off to scout. I walked the edge. I saw nothing, and then a gust of wind bulleted from the sky and shot across the water. The sound was there in the wind and whitecaps. I walked back to the canoe, pushed off, and continued paddling. I realized I needed to doubt every instinct I had.

23

The sun rose and began warming the day. I set up the tent at the base of a rocky esker where the river cut an eddy into the soft sandstone bank. Holly lay weighted down beneath the bank in cold water, the tether staked to shore. I spread antibiotic ointment onto the blisters of my hands that had broken open, the skin torn like restless bedsheets, my palms smeared with dried blood. I crawled into the tent and sleeping bag. I was so tired, but it seemed forever until I finally fell asleep.

I woke when I heard rustling outside the tent, like an animal scrounging for food. I quietly crawled to the tent flap and pulled the zipper one clicked tooth at time. Between me and the shoreline, less than a hundred feet away, stood a grizzly pawing through the top of the food pack with the cookstove and all the lunch supplies. For minutes I just watched as the bear buried its snout in the canvas. It came out with a gob of yellow cheese hanging from its jaws. The bear's head was the width of its shoulders, like the one I'd seen before with the dead musk ox, a male. His coat was sun-bleached gray with a silver streak that defined his humped back. The bear's snout sunk into the pack for more. Eventually, I knew he'd destroy the pack, then find the other. Then maybe Holly. I shouted as loud as I could, "Hey, hey, hey."

The bear snapped his head toward the tent and stood to his full height of eight feet. I yelled again. The bear dropped to all fours, then put his teeth into the pack and began dragging it backward. I kept shouting, and now the bear lifted the eighty-pound pack in his mouth like it was no heavier than a pillow. I stepped from the tent, picked up a rock, and pulled out a tin pot from the other pack. I banged the pot and followed the bear as he walked farther down the riverbank, then climbed the esker. I ran behind and kept banging, the bear now moving faster and pausing intermittently to look back. My anger was overwhelming—I wanted that pack, I needed that pack, and I'd wrestle the grizzly and get it back if it came to that. The bear was just over the top of the esker, stopped and watching. I kept banging and moving closer until I was a stone's throw away. Then he dropped the pack. For a second the bear paused—fight, flight, or freeze. He stepped cautiously toward me. He was so close I could smell him, and what I visualized were autumn leaves—he smelled like the fallen leaves in October just after a rain. The thought was incongruous next to the deeper fear overwhelming me. He kept coming. Then the bear made a quick charge, legs and feet in full gallop. For that split second, I froze, ready to be mauled. The bear stopped suddenly, maybe now as scared of me as I was of him, confused. I threw the rock in my hand and it landed on his snout. His head snapped back, stunned. I reached down for another rock, held it, and began slowly walking backward. I remembered the pilot's story of the grizzly, how the boy talked to it softly as though it were a dog. I said, "Nice bear, good bear." He watched me as I moved backward, and now I could see the hair on its back stand up like a mean dog ready to bite. He made a quick lunge, then stopped. I stood still, and he made another feigned lunge. The pilot, Knute, had given us his bear spray, a tall aerosol can of hot pepper extract that Holly had stowed at the bottom of her P-pack. It was useless to me now. Again, I moved slowly backward, maintaining eye contact, talking softly. The bear finally turned and walked toward the dropped pack. I turned also, and ran.

The bear spray was there in the pack. I wanted to empty the can in the grizzly's snout—I wanted my stuff back. I walked toward the esker, the bear spray held in front of me with my hand on the trigger and the safety clasp off. But the bear and the food pack were gone.

I quickly packed up, my hands shaking uncontrollably. I loaded the canoe and waded into the cold water to pull Holly from the river. The sleeping bag was soaked and heavy. Lifting her over the gunnel was a struggle, pulling and pushing her weight into the boat. I got her in and tethered, then started paddling downstream. The sun was past its zenith and the temperature was still warm, but I had to keep moving, get as far from the grizzly as possible.

I mentally inventoried the lost pack. It contained all the lunch supplies—the cheese, rye crackers, salami, peanut butter, and over fifteen pounds of trail mix. It held the stove and fuel to cook most of the food in the one pack I still had—the rice, pasta, freeze-dried vegetables, textured vegetable protein (TVP), oatmeal, pancakes, powdered eggs, tea, and coffee. I wasn't eating much and didn't care about the lost food right then—my fight was all base instinct—but I knew I would later.

All I could imagine now is what would've happened if the bear had found Holly.

24

I passed a place on the map called Grassy Island. There was no grass, only chest-high willows and swamp. Blackflies were out and I zipped the netting over my face. Along the length of the island I counted eight moose—two bulls, four cows, two calves. They lifted their heads above the willows as I canoed. Canada geese, snow geese, mergansers, pintails, and others weaved along the shores, probably nesting nearby—waterfowl I'd watched before on their migration through Nebraska.

The current moved slowly in the broad arcs of the river. The wind had calmed from the night before. I was still dead tired, but the stillness settled my mind. I no longer followed strange reflections or the illusions of impending rapids.

I knew Holly couldn't hear me in the bow of the canoe, I knew she wouldn't ever hear me again, but I wanted to continue telling my story of growing up with Jake on the Platte River—I felt compelled to. I knew she would've wanted to hear my stories as we camped along the Thelon—she would have loved me for it. I talked out loud to her as I paddled.

"Jake was once a different man, one who came from a society I'd only read about, a culture you probably lived. I saw a few pictures of his life back in Connecticut. In one photo, he had long, light brown hair with bangs that brushed his eyebrows. He wore a tennis shirt with an alligator logo and white tennis shorts. He had the same half-smile, confident, like he had all the answers to the world's problems. In the photo, he was plump, almost cherubic. The year I was born, Jake turned forty and he'd lost whatever fat he'd put on as a privileged youngster. He kept his uncut graying hair in a ponytail and grew a scraggly fuck-you beard. On his back was a shoulder to shoulder tattoo of the ouroboros, the snake biting its tail. Hence, Jake the Snake.

"He called himself an eco-anarchist, which is where the fringes of society, the no-government libertarians and the leftist back-to-nature hippies meet. I guess where the serpent head of society bites its tail. But to Jake, the ouroboros was a symbol of cyclical renewal, being close to the earth, the fertility of life and death in nature. He didn't believe in government or taxes. Self-sufficiency was being close to God, though he didn't believe in God. He believed in the earth as one organic being, and humanity was the cancer in that being. He wanted no part of the cancer, and his lifestyle was a choice not to participate.

"When I was five, Jake didn't enroll me in school—he didn't want my mind poisoned. And every day there'd be his lessons. He taught me how to read and write, and he taught me numbers. He went to the library in town and took out children's books. I also learned how to plant the garden, weed, and harvest. He had me memorize every tree, plant, mushroom, mammal, reptile, fish, and bird along the Platte. I still instinctively name a thing when I see it. We worked together on canning, and we fed and slaughtered the chickens and goats. We had a canoe on the river that we used to catch catfish and hunt ducks. He did work for others but usually bartered his labor for things we needed. I rarely saw paper money, but he kept a stash hidden in the cavity of a hollowed-out duck decoy. He needed cash for things like fuel and property taxes. But he ignored traffic tickets. He never renewed the plates on his truck, and the Columbus police wrote him a citation. I had just turned seven.

"A squad car came onto our property to execute a bench warrant. At the time, we were in the garden pulling onions, and I think if he had the chance, Jake would've gone for his handgun and started shooting. Jake always wore his holstered gun when on the property. But I was beside him, and Jake had no choice but to stand by me and say to the police, 'What is it you want?' They said they had a warrant for his arrest and to get on the ground with his hands behind his back. Jake just stood there, and the two policemen kept coming. I could see both unsnap their holsters and touch the handles of their handguns. I'm sure they weren't unaccustomed to government-hating freaks, and Jake looked the part. They told Jake again to get down on the ground—they were yelling—and I remember being frightened and crying. Jake finally did what they said, lay down on the ground with his face against the garden dirt. The policemen cuffed his wrists then led him to the back of the squad car.

"It was just a traffic ticket and a simple bench warrant. He'd be in the county jail for a night, in front of the judge the next day, then out with his pledge to pay. But there I was, seven years old, a little girl dressed as a boy, in secondhand clothing, and alone. The police couldn't leave me, so they waited for someone from Protective Services to come and pick me up. I sat there for hours, waiting and crying. I could see the silhouette of Jake in the squad car, but I couldn't talk to him or hear him. Finally, a lady came and took me away. I spent the next week in foster care on some farm in the hills north of town. Jake was out the day after his arrest and desperately trying that week to get me back.

"What I didn't know at the time was that the lady from Protective Services was now concerned for my welfare. Jake had no means of support, we lived in the basement of an unfinished house, no mother present, and I wasn't enrolled in school. She made a report to the county. Jake had to answer questions—and make promises.

"After that, living with Jake was different. The arrest scared him. I'm sure the city officials threatened to remove his child from the bunker. Jake loved me, and I didn't know what he'd do if I were taken away.

"I was enrolled in first grade that fall. I was two years older than most of the kids. I could already read and write, and I knew my multiplication tables. A month later they moved me up to third grade to be with the kids my age. But I'd rarely been around other kids, and I didn't know how to act. I felt anxious and withdrawn, and I was mostly left alone. I still feel that way around others.

"We'd have a visit once a month from the Protective Services lady. Jake followed her recommendation to apply for food stamps. He did work for others, but now only for cash money. He paid off his traffic ticket and bought current plates for the truck.

"Did his beliefs change? Did he become part of the cancer? I think he did what was needed to keep me. Honestly, if I hadn't been there, he would have gone down fighting rather than compromise. But there I was. They put a scare into him. We still took a deer off-season when needed, we played the alone game, and we still lived off the grid. He found other ways to make money without collecting a regular paycheck."

Past Grassy Island the river narrowed and the current became swifter. I paddled lightly, mostly to rudder, steering the canoe through the bends. The sun dropped below the trees and the temperature dropped with it. I kept paddling through the gloaming. I saw my first caribou standing alone at the river's edge drinking. It scented me first, then saw me, a lifting and turning of the head like any deer I'd tracked along the Platte. It moved carefully back into the cover of trees. I heard two wolves howling in the distance, speaking to each other, and I howled with them. It was another language—the Barrens another place I needed to fit in, like school when I was seven, like college at seventeen. But I was more at home here, and I felt unself-conscious talking to Holly and the wolves, no judgment of who I was.

25

By the morning I'd traveled over twenty miles to reach Hornby Point on the map. A cairn marked the site where the three men had died of starvation. I pulled over to unload the canoe where others had camped. I found slack water nearby and rested Holly beneath. I soaked oatmeal with sugar until it was edible. Laying in the tent, I counted the days. Holly had fallen on day twelve, and I guessed eighteen or nineteen since we'd left Yellowknife.

I slept briefly. When I woke, the temperature was still above sixty and too warm to pull Holly from the icy water. I walked the path toward Hornby's cabin not far from shore. It had been almost a hundred years since the three starved, and now the cabin had decayed to a rectangle of rotted log walls standing no higher than my waist. Holly had said it was the size of a one-car garage. To me it was like our chicken coop back in Nebraska. Three men, two my age, starving all winter long in this cabin, and I tried to imagine the insanity that took over their minds as they slowly died, the desperation to find anything to eat—boiled hides, rotting fish guts. Holly had said that the one boy kept a diary, that it was stashed in the stove with a note nearby, "Look in the stove." And I looked within the rectangle of rotting logs for the stove, then in the surrounding woods. What I did find were three marked graves, three wooden crosses held up by mounds of rocks. Hand-carved plaques were nailed to the center of each cross with the initials just barely legible, E.C., J.H., H.A. One wooden cross was broken and missing much of the crosspiece. In front of each were new crosses that someone had carved to replace the rotting ones. I thought of Holly. I could leave her here, dig a grave, cover her with rocks, and make a cross with her initials. She'd be in a place she loved, and I could come back to the Barrens each summer to visit her grave and remember her short life. Rebuild her cross when I returned. The idea was comforting, but I wasn't ready to leave her.

I sat by the graves while I waited for the temperature to drop. My mind drifted back to Nebraska. I wanted to talk about Jake and continue telling my story to Holly—and maybe the three beneath the markers.

"We always grew a few pot plants in the state forest out by the Platte. The area would flood every few years and the soil was rich in nutrients. Jake called it ditch weed and would smoke it most evenings before going to bed. It wasn't a big deal. Then one year Jake traded with our neighbors, Guatemalans, for the weed they'd bought from other migrants in town. The town weed was more potent, nothing like the ditch weed Jake had grown for years, and Jake somehow got hold of the seeds. He planted more weed and replaced the old pot with the more potent stuff.

"I was fifteen and in high school. I kept to myself and spent more time with teachers than other kids. But there was a boy I was friends with, his name was Cody. It's funny, we met when I was twelve. I was like an outcast, the first girl in class to have boobs, and then I had big ones. Cody had the hots for me, and one time after school I was cornered behind a dumpster. Within seconds his tongue was down my mouth with his hands fondling my tits. I tried to like it—it's what I thought I was supposed to do. But honestly, I just didn't, and I pushed him away. I said, 'Get the fuck off me,' and he did. It's funny because we became friends after that. I'm sure he knew I was gay, but it was something we didn't discuss. We talked more about hunting, knives and guns, our families, or kids at school. We'd sometimes hang out at a campsite along the Platte, a place I could walk to after dinner. I'd bring weed from Jake's stash, and we'd get high. One thing led to another. Cody wanted to know if I could get him more weed. We had trash bags full of the stuff in the loft of an outbuilding. I brought him a half-pound and Cody sold most of it to his friends. Cody gave me a cut, and I supplied more weed. But then Jake found out.

"On the angry meter, Jake the Snake could hit a solid ten. Anger was his base emotion. He was angry at society, vowing that he'd never be a slave to it. He was angry at technology, convinced it was society's tool to enslave him. Ironically, he had an old car radio with a cassette player that he'd wired into our batteries, and he'd listen to the local NPR station or sometimes Rush Limbaugh on the local fascist talk station. He'd get all worked up and start a rant, yelling at the radio, how they were all wrong, how the world was all fucked-up. He'd slam his fist onto the kitchen table or kick at the cinder-block walls. In a twisted way, the radio fed his anger and, I think, gave him masochistic pleasure. One time I asked him why he didn't just turn the thing off and stop listening. He looked at me all crazy, and I thought then that he might snap and hit me. All he said was, 'Shut the fuck up.'

"Jake confronted me about the weed one night over dinner. I could see the anger in his jaw, in the way he gnashed his teeth, and I could tell he was doing everything he could to control his temper. He knew how much I'd taken, that I couldn't smoke that much in a year, and knew I was doing something with Cody. He asked what was going on, and I told him, 'Cody is selling the weed to kids at school.' For minutes he just sat there silently staring at his food. Then his arm swiped across the table, sending his plate of meat and potatoes flying. More silence. He couldn't look up to meet my eyes, but I could tell he was calming down, thinking. Then he asked how much I was making? I told him Cody was paying me about ten dollars an ounce. He said, 'Cody is ripping you off.'

"He'd always traded or sold our surplus vegetables, and it wasn't a stretch for him to sell the weed. Jake didn't believe that drugs should be illegal. But what he wanted was reasonable compensation for his weed. The next time I met Cody, Jake was there. He said straight out, 'The deal is, I get ten dollars per *quarter*-ounce, and that's a better deal than you'll get from any Latino in town. You two can sell the quarter ounces for twenty.'

"Cody nodded his head. It was okay with him.

"I didn't know beforehand that Jake was now sticking me on the illegal, selling end of the deal. Fucking Jake. I don't know if he realized it then or just didn't care, but he was putting me in danger."

26

By the time the Arctic night descended, the birch and spruce of the oasis had slowly vanished, and I was back to the barrenness of the tundra. I kept slicing my paddle through the water, moving like the water itself to take another stroke. Instead of the cumbersome J-stroke, I'd taken to paddling three strokes on one side, then three on the other. Holly was not there to tell me if what I was doing was wrong, lazy, or maybe even more efficient. It felt more efficient, and I kept paddling that way. My blisters stung, but they'd stopped bleeding. A ridge of calluses had begun to form where the pads of my fingers curled over the paddle handle. I'd toughed it out.

I started to see caribou, alone or in small groups. I breathed rhythmically and quietly through my nose. None seemed frightened of the sole paddler, and none looked up to acknowledge my passing. I felt like a ghost, and part of me wanted to make my presence known, find a reflection of my existence in this land.

The anxiety I was used to wasn't there, and I had this feeling that my body was not my body. My arms felt detached and moved autonomously as though controlled by another being. My breathing was not my own, and the aches I felt in my knees or shoulders were objectified in my mind like I imagined the phantom pain of an amputated limb. A single musk ox looked up as I passed, and I could see what it saw, a strange being crossing the river ferrying a dead body to the other world.

I blinked my eyes and shook my head to pull out of the lucid dream. I touched my upper paddle hand to my nose and readjusted my knees on the sleeping pad. I exhaled forcefully through my mouth to hear the whoosh sound and see the puff of condensation in the cool air. I needed to eat more. I didn't have an appetite, but I felt light-headed and sensed emptiness in my stomach.

I was also lonely. I was so tired of being lonely. As I paddled through the night, I talked to Holly. The act of telling a story felt comforting like I could imagine something or someone out there who could hear me and acknowledge my presence.

"A farmer's kid nearby bought an off-road motorcycle and started tearing down the trails of the state forest. The sound was a loud chainsaw whine that could be heard for miles. Jake wrote an anonymous letter to the County Sheriff's office complaining—I think hoping they would do something before he did. A month later the kid was still tearing through the woods. Then one day I heard the motorcycle, then nothing, and then screaming for help. I ran toward the sound deep in the forest. I saw the kid lying there still screaming, one arm motionless in the dirt. I knew right off it was broken. The bike was behind him with its front fork and wheel bent backward. Behind that, I saw the deep hole dug in the trail. I tied a sling with the kid's T-shirt and then helped him home. When I confronted Jake—he could have killed the kid—he just said, 'Shut the fuck up.' I think his only respite from pure anger, from going off the deep end completely and sending Unabomber-type explosives through the mail, was me. I was the only source of love in his life to offset his anger.

"Another time, the spring of my sophomore year, I was almost popular, though that's not the right word. People knew me—I was the girl who sold weed. The campsite out on the Platte became a thing, and on Friday nights kids showed up and sometimes partied until the sun rose. I knew Jake was concerned, nervous, and he warned me over and over about the kids I hung out with and what I might become. But he'd already pushed me to become a drug dealer—it was his usual fucked-up hypocrisy. I went out to the river parties regardless. I knew he wouldn't leave me be, and I sensed him out in the woods at night watching.

"One time, a boy brought a handgun out to the river with a box of cartridges, and the kids traded off shooting empty beer cans and liquor bottles. I knew the boy from school, a real asshole. He was on the wrestling team, made all-conference his sophomore year, and was expected to go to state his junior year. His parents named him Jericho, like the city in the Bible. His thing was crystal meth, and he'd do it to keep his weight class. So now he was tweaking and waving the gun around, and Cody told him to knock it off and put the thing away. Jericho got all serious and sinister. He stared at Cody, his eyes unblinking with swollen dark irises like bullet holes. He leveled the gun at Cody and pulled back the hammer. He smiled. We were all quiet, Cody staring down Jericho, and Jericho looking crazed. Jericho said, 'What, motherfucker?'

"And Cody said, 'You heard me.'

"That's when Jake came out of the woods. He stepped slowly, and we could all hear the crunching sound of his boots on twigs.

Knowing Jake, he *wanted* us to hear. So now Jericho turned his gun toward the sound of someone in the woods. I heard Jake beyond the light of the fire. He said, 'Boy, you'd better put that gun down, I've got a thirty-ought-six aimed at your head. You've got three seconds.' He counted, 'One . . .' And then Jericho carefully released the hammer and put the gun down and turned his palms up to show his hands. Real cowboy-like. Jake came out from the shadows with his hunting rifle butted against his hip and moved around the fire to Jericho. He picked up the handgun, flipped on the safety, and tucked it into his waistband. All with one hand while he held his rifle. He told Jericho to come see him at the house if he wanted his gun back. Never once did he look at me, and later what he said was, 'Those river parties are over.' I guess that was obvious. Who'd want to show up at the river or anywhere else where they knew my psycho father would be out in the woods, watching everything we did. I loved Jake, but I could hate him too. Telling these stories, thinking about the fucked-up way he raised a child, I sometimes hate him now. There was one more.

"Our neighbors were from Guatemala, and two brothers worked at the Behlen plant turning steel into grain elevators. For several years they'd invited Jake and me over for their Mayan New Year's celebration that came every 260 days. Jake and the brothers drank Famosa beer while I helped their wives prepare a meal of chicken stewed with tomatillos and cilantro and thickened with pumpkin seeds, sesame seeds, and tortillas. They had five kids who showed me how to play a game of marbles called *cincos*. We lit fireworks at night. It was like the imagined family I never had.

"Then one day, one of their goats got loose and strayed onto our land and Jake killed it. Fences lined the Guatemalans' property on the two sides that bordered roads, so the goat had to have strayed onto our yard or into the state forest. By the time the two brothers came by, Jake had butchered the goat. He told them he hadn't seen it, which they knew was a lie. After that, we never received another invitation for their New Year's celebration. I counted the 260 days and I waited. I heard the fireworks. Jake just said, 'Shut the fuck up.'"

THE GLOAMING CREATED an eerie moonscape of low sweeping hills with undulating textures of crushed rock and sand. I heard a wolf howl, and I howled back and the wolf howled again, *I'm out here, I heard you, and you're not alone.*

I kept on with my stories. There was one that no one witnessed.

"Fall of my junior year Cody started selling Oxys along with the weed Jake grew. He gave me one to try, and I took it at lunchtime. It hit me quick, and I dream-walked through my last classes. I felt detached in a way that was soothing. The anxiety I had around studying, getting A's, Jake, my sexuality, fell away like they were all inconsequential. The teachers talked, and I sat back and just heard the words that floated around my head like moths. It wasn't like I was introspective in any way—it wasn't like I consciously didn't care—it was more that nothing existed outside the nothingness shroud that surrounded me.

"After Jake crashed the party at the river, the kids were scared of me. I was still the girl with the weed, but I was also the girl with the father who crept around and knew everything that was going on. Cody still dealt, but I only sold to a few desperate customers, mostly guys who were too stoned to be scared or freshman girls that didn't know any better.

"Now, here's something I want to say, but I don't want you to think that I'm a coward, because I'm anything but a coward. I knew kids talked about me. I've known I liked women since I was like eleven. I didn't act on it then and I only acted on it once in high school. I sensed one other woman liked me—this was right before the incident with the handgun—and we became friends. Her name was Sarah, and we started hanging out together between classes. Then one day in the restroom, when I knew we'd be alone, I kissed her. Stupid. She kissed me back, I swear, but then she quickly left to go to class. Sarah avoided me after that. And after that, I knew there was talk. A couple times I heard things behind my back like, 'Fucking dyke.' The asshole, Jericho, did the V thing with his fingers, flicking his tongue in and out, then smiled like it was all a big joke. But I didn't think of myself as a victim, someone who felt sorry for themselves because they were different. Then again, sometimes I'd just pop an Oxy, zone out, and make it all go away. Funny, in a way I was that girl *you* outed in sixth grade. What was her name? Yeah, Tonya.

"And Jake? Jake liked different—he didn't want me to be a girly-girl, someone who went out on dates, someone who went to prom, someone who straightened her hair and made her lips all fruity red. I think he thought of me as a tomboy and just not interested in doing the whole high school thing. Jake wanted me in his world for himself, and the more I stayed away from others, the more it pleased him. Jake thought he was molding me into a person like himself that rejected society. What he didn't understand was that I was rejecting it all—high school and his world—for what *I* wanted. I knew I was different.

"One day I snapped. It wasn't any one thing—I don't remember being bullied or kids talking behind my back. What I remember is a sense of loneliness. It hit me hard that I was different and that I'd never know anyone like me, or anyone who would truly love me for who I was. One day I guess I was profoundly depressed and feeling sorry for myself, feeling like a coward. So I bought a handful of Oxys from Cody, like eight or ten—I can't remember the exact number. That evening I sat on the edge of my bed. The decision was not a conscious one, more like an impulse. I sucked the side of my mouth and collected a reservoir of saliva, then swallowed the pills. I lay back on my bed and thought about my life, my shitty life living off the grid in the bunker with Jake and going to school with kids I didn't know. And then I started to cry. I realized that I'd miss it all anyway and I was sad to be ending it. I felt the Oxys take hold of my mind—the apathy of the drug. And then I fell asleep.

"I had this vivid dream, a vision. I was out at the river with Cody and the other kids. We sat around the fire, and everyone was smoking a joint, passing it around, but each time the joint came my way, it passed by me like I didn't exist. I was invisible. I tried to touch the girl next to me, someone who I'd never seen before, but my fingers pushed right through her. She couldn't feel my touch, and she wouldn't acknowledge my presence. Then I floated up like a balloon and looked down on everyone around the fire. I could feel the heat from the burning wood and see the kids talking and laughing, and I could see myself there by the fire staring ahead, removed from the rest. And I could see Jake watching me. Then I floated farther up until the fire was a speck of light, and in the distance I could see the lights of town. I rose higher, and now the earth was just clusters of lights amid larger areas of total blackness. Then I woke up.

"I was overwhelmed with relief because I was still alive.

"I knew what the dream meant, and it *was* a vision. I knew that these weren't my people, not even Jake. I knew there existed another world with dots of light that *were* my people and that I'd need to move out, move away, to find them. I'd keep my head down and finish high school. I would leave after graduation, to college or wherever, find out who else was in this world. I'd leave Jake and never look back. I'd find you."

27

The colors of the landscape changed as the sun traveled back above the horizon. The water turned emerald green in places, then azure. The green of the shrubs became vibrant against the darker lichen and the rocky eskers. The few clouds turned billowy white against the washed-blue sky. I knew I needed to stop and put Holly beneath the Thelon, eat, and sleep. The river flowed around a sandbar island. I chose the side that looked deepest and pulled up to the island where an eddy of slack water formed. I heard two wolves howling and howled with them.

Inside the tent I felt a headache coming on, faint, but I knew it would grow as the barometer dropped. I fell asleep waiting for the impending storm.

I woke up in the afternoon. My headache was a full-blown assault on the sinuses between my eyes. Outside, hail was pelting the tent canopy. It sounded like someone whipping the tent with a stick, Dene hunters again. The hail turned to rain, and I felt the floor of the tent turn soggy. I crawled out of the sleeping bag and packed it so that it stayed dry. I pulled on my Muck Boots and sat on the sleeping pad rolled up. The rain stopped, but the wind continued to gust from the west. I stepped out from the tent and found a sandstone ledge, a windbreak. I ate a soup of pancake mix and powdered eggs, and felt the energy of the meal immediately, like a drug. I packed up the soggy tent and the rest of the gear and loaded the canoe. I lifted the weights off Holly. Her cocooned body ascended in the shallow water, either bubbles trapped in the folds of the sleeping bag, or bloat. I didn't detect any smell. The wind was mostly at my back, and I put more miles behind me, closer to Baker Lake.

The dusk and semidarkness of the Arctic night were made stranger by the howls of wolves along the river that would answer my call. I started to know the different sounds, the inflection of howls. Some seemed lonely, just an acknowledgment that another being was out there. Others were playful like two people singing in the night. I kept looking on the shore and around the next bend to see who I was communing with, but none appeared. Sometimes I thought the conversation was another lucid dream, a hallucination, that what I heard was just a voice in my head that sought its own comfort. What I needed was to see one of my wolf companions. Around another bend the wolf howl was close, very close, and I stopped to find out if I had a real companion.

I pulled the canoe up to shore. The night was as dark as it gets—light from deep beneath the horizon that showed the silhouette of the land with its grayish details locked in shadows. I howled and the wolf howled back, and I walked inland toward the sound. My eyes adjusted to the shadows. Being there reminded me of when I'd tracked the deer—the blood only discernible because it glistened. I crossed an esker of gravelly rock that slid under my boots. On the other side I howled again and followed the reply that seemed to come from farther down the lee side. And then I saw the wolf, just a blur of movement as it slipped into a hole under the esker. I stopped and waited. Then I made the howl sound I thought was playful. The wolf stepped from the hole, the den, and returned my howl. I saw now that the wolf was white. I crawled forward, hoping to get closer, and I could see the light reflected in the wolf's eyes and see it scent the air. Then I heard a different sound, a yip from the den, and I knew the wolf was a bitch, a mother, and she'd borne a pup. I wanted to be close, and I kept crawling nearer. I crested a small ridge and peeked over the top. The wolf stood a hundred feet from me now, could probably smell me, but just watched. I made a playful sound, a high-pitched howl with sudden inflections.

I saw the pup's head poke out from the den and look around curiously. I made the sound again, and now the pup made a similar sound back. The mother dropped to her stomach and nuzzled the neck of the pup who crawled out and stood looking for its new companion. I howled playfully again, and now the pup dashed toward the sound, toward where I lay behind the ridge. The mother jumped up then and caught the pup by the neck before it could leave her safety. She lifted the pup and dropped it back in the den. A simple scene—a mother and her child, a child like Holly's Theo. At that moment I ached for her and what might have been. I crawled backward, away from the mother wolf, her pup, and their den.

I walked back to the canoe and pushed off onto the river once more. The dusk light was getting brighter, and the new day would start soon. It was colder since the storm, and I kept paddling for a few more hours. Midmorning, I stopped on a shore where the water was slack. I'd not heard a wolf since I left the den.

I untied and lifted Holly from the canoe and slid her body into the cold river. The three lengths of rope with six weights were looped around my neck, and I placed them across her legs, waist, and torso. Afterward, I hiked up the gradual slope of the riverbank to the highest point. I could see for miles and there was no sign of other humans. There was no one on this fucking river but us.

28

Inside the tent I pulled out Holly's guitar and tried the chords I knew. There was a song in the chords, but it hadn't come to me yet, and the thought of singing just made me sad. Her phone was at the bottom of her P-pack, and since the accident, I hadn't touched it. Now I wanted to. I wanted to see Holly's face and feel the memories triggered by photos. I knew her password, but when I turned it on, a low battery message appeared and the screen went blank. I attached the phone to the solar charger and laid both just outside the tent.

Before I slept, I thought of the wolf and the pup, the mother and her offspring, Holly and Theo. I imagined a story like Holly had envisioned with the story of Theo. I added to her story, our story, and I let it come alive in my conscious mind, ideas rising like bubbles from deep beneath the river's surface—who we were, what happened that made our lives together unique, and what we discovered that made our lives more complete. Like Holly had done, I went through each detail in my head before I said it out loud.

"By the time we graduate, we're a couple and we've moved in together. It's just a small one-bedroom apartment, and like you said, proximity amplifies our love.

"After college you're accepted into an MFA writing program in Iowa. I follow you there because you asked me to, and I've got no other place to go, certainly not back to Nebraska. I have a mathematics degree from Brown, but, frankly, I just don't know what I want in life outside of you. We find an apartment, and you start school. I get a job working for a cabinet maker, and every day I learn more about working with wood. I find I like working with my hands and making things. Touching things, molding things is real and familiar. I feel grounded.

"After finishing the MFA program, you find a job working as an associate professor at a small college in Saint Paul. It's near where you grew up and close to your parents. Since our trip through the Barrens, you've told your parents everything about yourself and me. You tell them we're in love, and you ask them to accept who we are. After a time, they do. Your father likes me because we drink beer together and talk about old cars and camping. It takes a while for your mother to come around. She's had this vision that you'd get married to a man and have your wedding at the country club where her friends and relatives show up and say what a beautiful couple they make, how smart they both are, and what a bright future they'll have. It's something she's always latched on to, but now the vision, the fantasy, is crushed. Would the club even allow a same-sex wedding? Could she put her friends through that? But what's her alternative? Is she ready to push you away, disown you? Eventually she accepts what is and learns to manage her expectations, finding that I'm not nasty or threatening, that I'm okay. And thank God Holly and I don't want a wedding at the club. But we do get married, just a small ceremony at an old Saint Paul mansion. You wear a white cocktail dress, while I wear a black suit and tie with a long, tailored coat that covers my big ass and thighs. I think I look good.

"You start telling stories, first writing short stories that get published locally. You play your guitar and tell stories at open mics around town. Some of them are about the two of us on the Thelon. Then one short story gets accepted by a national magazine with a wide circulation. You receive notes from interested literary agents.

"You write your first book, a historical novel based on the Hornby story of starvation and death on the Thelon. For your research we travel back to the Thelon and repeat the trip we'd done years before. We spend a week at Hornby Point, and you try to understand how they lived, how they ate, talked, hunted, gathered, and kept warm. I'm there with you, and I show you how they lived because that's how I lived growing up. I know how to hunt, gather, keep warm. I know what it's like to live without the comforts and entertainment that comes with electricity and Wi-Fi. You understand me even better after the trip is done, and you use that to bring the novel to life, make it real. The book is published.

"There's a book signing party at a local boxing gym. There are no naked lesbians in the ring and no graphic photos behind a line of punching bags. The place, though, is packed with friends, relatives, colleagues, students, critics—lots of people. You give a brief reading and then tell stories of your times on the Thelon. There's champagne, wine, beer, and food. Your mother had a cake made to rival anything at a country club wedding. I've never seen you so happy, so proud. And I've had one of my woodwork restorations featured in a local magazine. I learn what it's like to arrive, to be accepted by a community of professionals—the recognition. The Hornby book is that times ten, and I'm just so proud of you. There's a DJ and dancing in the boxing ring that goes on past midnight. We dance with each other and with everyone. You're so happy. And we stay around until there's only the two of us in the gym. We're quiet, and I let you just feel the aura of the long evening. You turn to me then and say, 'Let's have a baby, that would complete us.'

"I just say, 'Yeah.'"

The story was finished—the life that could have been, what I thought Holly would have imagined. It felt real, like maybe it did happen. And that tangible feeling of the story, what could have been, pulled tears from my eyes and I let out a faint cry, chokes of air from deep down. I grieved—*I miss her so much.*

29

The temperature had cooled by the time I woke. The cell phone was probably charged, but I couldn't bring myself to look at the photos. I got back on the river and paddled through the sunset. All around was a glowing landscape of sand and gravel. There was water everywhere, but it felt like a desert. Then I saw a patch of green with small white six-pointed flowers, Arctic starflower, and patches of low shrubs and other flowers. I took in the whole landscape like Holly had taught me, felt myself a part of it like I was just another animal passing in the Arctic night. I stopped and laid my paddle across the gunwales. In the silence I felt the cold wind against my nose and cheeks. The canoe moved with the slow current, and I heard ripples of water lapping against the rocky shore like distant wind chimes. I touched the water and brought a handful against my face. I felt immersed, and part of me was comforted with the thought of dying here, peacefully decomposing, then emerging as something else, with Holly.

I paddled until the sun climbed back above the horizon, paddled until the temperature started to rise, and wanted to keep paddling but knew I couldn't. I found the next shallow eddy where I could rest Holly.

The thought of water against my face was still with me, and I walked to the water's edge and undressed. I stood naked and cold. The water was freezing, and I went in fast, first stepping out into deeper water then falling forward and sinking my whole body beneath the moving river. I came up startled for air and then went down again. Blood rushed to my skin and for a moment it felt good to be underwater. The current pushed me back, and I held on to rocks at the bottom. I thought of Holly taking that first breath of water as she tumbled in the undertow of the rapids. Was it panic or some kind of acceptance? I wanted to know and I wanted to take a breath, open my mouth, and fill my lungs with water. I imagined panic, then acceptance. A longing to have my life over with, to be done and at peace. I wanted the immersion, the acceptance—it would be so easy. A deeper instinct forced my head above water. I remembered the handful of Oxys I took in high school, the thought taking hold that I'd miss it all, and then the overwhelming feeling of being alive. I knew that alive I could still be with Holly. I gulped for air.

Walking back to shore, I touched the exposed gash on my forehead. It was deep and splintered. The edges were sore but firm, and I was sure there was no infection. The gash would leave a scar like a fat pink leech, a memento of the Thelon. I dried myself with Holly's towel. It was the first time I'd used it. I looked at the towel's pattern, a beach scene with a Corona bottle and lime. The words across the top said, "Find Your Beach." I smiled, thinking about Holly and her ironic towel. Maybe I *would* find my beach. I rewrapped my forehead with sugar, just a few more days until I could leave it to dry and scab over.

Later in the tent I did open her phone and look through the pictures. The first photo was the selfie. The image stood out crystal clear, her startled face. I looked at it and then looked away. With Holly's body wrapped in the sleeping bag and out of sight, I could almost convince myself that what had happened wasn't real, and I could imagine it was just me, paddling with no consequences of an accident, a death. The photo was a memory I wanted to expunge, and I pressed the trash-can symbol. The DELETE PHOTO button appeared—a second chance—and I paused. I knew it wasn't that easy; I couldn't erase what had happened. I hit the CANCEL button below. The next photo showed her standing on the bluff, smiling with her practiced smile, the corners of her mouth stretched like rubber bands, her straw cowboy hat pulled down to her eyebrows—I should have looked for the hat. I posed in the next photo, minutes before she fell, smiling like nothing would happen. The smartphone organized the photos by place and date. The Thelon photos were under the heading, "Yellowknife," the last time the phone had connected to the internet and GPS. I scrolled through others—Saint Paul, Providence, Montreal, Winnipeg. I was in many—no practiced smile, hair like Spanish moss, jeans, then voluminous athletic shorts, and flannel. Her mother was exactly how Holly had described her—a hair helmet like Margaret Thatcher's, a trace of Holly's smile, her plump lips. Her father wore a white dress shirt with a button-down collar, his face tan, and Holly's nose. Her parents were in the story of us getting married and deciding to start a family. Holly was part of a family before I imagined her part of mine. Her parents deserved to see Holly again, and I would keep surviving so that they could.

30

I woke up and ate hydrated pancake mix with powdered eggs and the hard flakes of TVP. The TVP added no flavor that I could tell. The eggs left a chemical aftertaste. I ate what I could. I was losing weight, and my Carhartt pants hung loose from my hips.

As I took my first paddle stroke, I counted day twenty-one. At least, I thought it was day twenty-one. The current ran steady and swift and took me faster than I could paddle. I ruddered the canoe, following the dark blue of deep water. I'd seen signs of past canoers—firepits with ashes, a hole in the ground where someone had staked a tent, an energy bar wrapper carelessly left behind—but I'd been on the river for three weeks and not seen a soul. I felt that in the end I *would* get out of this place. I wasn't hurt, I still had food, and eventually I'd run into someone, or paddle the entire way to Baker Lake. Another accident could still happen, but somehow I knew I'd get back to civilization, and I'd be forced to confront whatever consequences waited for me. I wouldn't be lucky enough to avoid that inevitability.

My grief for Holly was there, continually simmering, and I knew that when I did get back, the grief would come bubbling up my spine and attack me like some maniac with a ball-peen hammer. And I'd be sharing that grief with her parents, who may or may not hold me accountable for what had happened. *What could I have done? Why did I survive?*

But for now, the grief floated beyond me, out with the wolves and caribou and bears and musk ox, flying with the geese, gyrfalcons, ptarmigans, and gulls. I felt like I couldn't touch it; I couldn't feel who I was anymore. I was just out in the ether of the wilderness, dipping my paddle and slicing through the water with a canoe, food and gear, a body—a purpose.

The river widened and the current slowed. The south shore was walled in by a sandstone bluff topped by purple lupines and crimson spikes of Indian paintbrush. I could smell them. I pulled off on the north shore and set up camp. I found driftwood at the top of the flood line and made a fire to cook a meal with vegetable soup mix, rice, and curry seasoning. It was the first hot meal I'd had since the accident. The flavor of Indian spice was shocking to my palate, and the warmth of the food comforted my whole body.

After cleaning up I pulled out the pack guitar and played the few chords I knew until I found the Dylan song, "Tangled Up in Blue," the song Jake had listened to over and over, the song Holly had played on her guitar. I found the melody as best I could and sang all seven verses. I realized that parts had been written in first person, some in third, some in present tense, some in past, some in future. Time and space and perception all jumbled together so that I felt everything or nothing could happen. I put the guitar back in its case. I laid another length of driftwood on the fire. I told Holly more about what happened to me in Nebraska.

"I wasn't naïve—I knew Jake needed and wanted sex. I figured that's what he did the times he left the house for a few days. He never told me where he went, just that he'd be gone and be back. Whatever, I could take care of myself from the time I was five. I thought, *Go ahead, Jake, get your freak on.* But then one day he showed up with Rose and her dog Rex. My mother's name was Ruby and the likeness didn't escape me. Did he bring someone back to mother me? I was seventeen and too old for that.

"Rose was originally from Tarzana in California. 'Named after Tarzan the ape man,' she said. But by the looks of her, she hadn't been back there for some time, or washed. Her hair had taken on the color of dried dirt, long and matted in places. Her various clothes were once a distinct color but now matched her hair. She wore laced high-top work boots with soles worn thin. Around her neck was a pink bandanna, the only shot of true color, probably washed in sinks, ponds, and streams when she could—her one expression of vanity. Her dog, Rex, was a German shepherd mix. His coat had the black and tan colorings of a shepherd but longer and fuller like a husky. The dog took an instant dislike to me and almost bit my hand off when I reached to pet it. Rose said, 'Rex doesn't take to some people.'

"Rose, though, did try to take to *me*. Right off, she hugged, then said how much she'd heard about me, how she thought we'd be so close. All during this, Jake stood behind her, looking elsewhere. He knew I'd be pissed, and later outside when I had him alone, I said, 'What the fuck, Jake?' He was never one for back talk, and I'd always done as he said. The property was his domain, and sometimes I felt like his hired hand. Don't get me wrong—I know Jake loved me. I did the work, but he also spent time caring for me, guiding me. I made it out of Columbus despite Jake, but also because of Jake. Anyway, he wasn't one for back talk, and he just said, 'Shut the fuck up.'

"I kept my distance over the next week. Rose wasn't much of a cook, but she ate our food and helped wash the dishes. After dinner I'd retreat to my small windowless room and close the hanging drapes that took the place of a door. While I did my homework, I could hear them talk politics. Jake was saying the same anarchist shit I'd listened to my entire life. It was a creed I understood but didn't want to follow. Rose, though, was a follower. She'd read the same books and believed the same stuff. And where Jake withdrew from society to live a simple life in the woods, Rose had been all across the country trying to make a difference—two Republican conventions, Occupy Wall Street, Rally Against Hate in Berkeley, and Unite the Right rally in Charlottesville. They'd get stoned, the smoke wafting into my room. Then I could hear their fucking.

"One night I just couldn't take it anymore. Jake was saying how the whole world was fucked, that civilization was moving toward self-destruction. Rose was all, 'I hear ya, yeah man, I know what you mean, it can't be stopped.' Then Jake was back to how the only way to stay alive and avoid the self-destruction was to live away from the techno society. Then Jake went further and said to Rose, 'You should live here with us.'

"I stood up, opened the curtain, and said, 'Jake, you need to shut the fuck up.'

"I don't know what I expected—I'd never used those same words against him. Jake looked at me, unblinking with his lips clamped tight. I could see that same twitch in his jaw, the gnashing whenever he got mad. I guess what Jake thought or felt was beyond words. He slapped me, a full-handed slap that came from his hip and crossed my face with a force that knocked me down.

"The dog, Rex, jumped at the show of violence. I heard a loud, 'Stop,' and Rex froze, looking at me with his teeth bared, making a low growl. Rose kept saying to Rex, 'It's okay, boy, it's okay, boy.' Maybe talking to Jake, too.

"I went into my room and gathered my homework, my quilt, pillow, and head lamp. I sidestepped the dog held tight by Rose and walked from the bunker. I spent that night in the hayloft. I stayed in the loft for the next two weeks and stayed away from Jake and Rose as much as I could. I ate lunch at the school cafeteria. I stuffed my backpack with leftover food for dinner or ate fast food in town. I continued selling Jake's weed, but all I could focus on was getting the fuck out of Columbus. I wanted to find *my* people."

31

I reached a place on the map called Lookout Point. The sun was climbing in the sky and the temperature rising. To keep Holly's body cool, it was time to stop for the day. The white sandbanks of the river sloped gradually up to a tundra field of green shrubs and lichen. I would not have stopped, as there didn't seem to be a high spot that I would call a lookout, but a cairn marked a campsite and trail.

I followed the trail to the top of the lookout. I was only fifty feet above the river, but the land was so flat and low to the water that I could see for miles, and what I saw was more of the same. Then I followed movement in the distance, a flock of white birds like a cloud moving up the river toward me. As they got closer, I could see their black markings, knife-blade wings, and long trailing feathers—like kites. At first I thought gulls, they sounded like gulls, but gulls didn't move like that, all jerky like sparrows or chickadees. They hovered over the river and I watched as they descended on a school of small fish. Their beaks were long, pointed, and orange. They sailed close to the surface to pick out the fish, then moved to the shore to eat. I knew the name of the bird, but there was no one to speak it to. And now the names no longer seemed important.

Soot-covered rocks of an ancient fire ring were near the top of the lookout, and I recognized that for the Dene this would've been a good place to camp, watch, and hunt. I walked back down to the cairn to bring up the packs. It was then I noticed the scraps of paper sticking from between the rocks, notes like the ones we'd seen before. I pulled one out and read, "Maya and Oscar—28th July 2016—Those who wish to sing, always find a song." Some proverb or quote, maybe sappy, but I connected with the sentiment. I put the scrap back and pulled out others. A few were Bible quotes. One said, "When he got to the boat, his disciples followed him." I knew it was a passage from the Book of Matthew, an appeal to the Israelites that Jesus was the chosen one. For me, Holly was the chosen one, and I followed *her*. Another note was just funny, "Don Juan—August 5, 2017—So fucking bored, can't wait to get back to NYC." Bored was not a term I'd use. Then I read one dated this year, August 1, 2019, "Voyager Trip, Camp Kawishiwi. Anne, Charlotte, Bean, Max." It was the camp Holly had gone to, and I knew it must be near that date now, but I didn't know the exact date for sure and my watch was an old military thing with hands. I thought of her cell phone in the P-pack. I booted up the phone and found the date, August 4. I was just three days behind this group. The thought that I could find help on the river was growing more tangible, and the adrenaline flowing through my body fed my excitement. I ran back up to the lookout and surveyed the landscape for any sign of smoke—anything. The flock of birds had moved on. I saw nothing in the distance, just the sand, rock, shrubs, and lichen of the Barrens. Water and nothing. But now I had real hope.

I took out the current map that I'd been following for the last week. It was sixty miles until the Thelon Bluffs, then the big lakes of Beverly, Aberdeen, Shultz, and finally the town of Baker Lake. Two hundred more miles with two hundred and fifty behind me. Hornby Point was sixty miles back and three days ago, so on the river I was doing twenty miles a day. Maybe the Kawishiwi group was doing the same. If I could bump it to thirty or more miles a day, then I might reach them in a week. I thought I could do that, paddle ahead of the current, stop to pee, eat, and sleep. Sleep only during the warmest parts of the day.

Holly was already submerged and the temperature was rising. Eat and sleep now and then start again toward evening. I set up the tent near the fire ring. I had no wood. I soaked oatmeal with freeze-dried vegetables but could only eat half. I slept lightly, waking up often to see the diffused light of the sun still illuminating the tent. I was up and dressed when I finally felt the temperature drop against my face. I packed the canoe and set off.

32

It rained periodically throughout the night. I stopped paddling to pull on Holly's waterproof parka that zipped uncomfortably tight to my chest. For hours, the clouds diffused the light from the sun that had settled below the horizon. I could still see the river but not much else. The Thelon continued to run wide and deep with few rocks and no whitewater. I just kept paddling, switching every three strokes as I moved the canoe through the long, arcing bends. I thought of a Jimmy Buffet song Jake and I had sung, "He Went to Paris." I knew the lyrics and story. It was about a man who went to Paris, married, had a family, and was content. Then he lost the wife and child to war and finally drifted away to the Caribbean. At the age of eighty-six, the man looks back on his life and sees the tragedy, but also the magic in what he experienced and felt. He knew that in spite of the tragic deaths of his wife and child, he had a good life. I sang, and it felt good to sing, and at the end I wondered if at the age of eighty-six, *I'd* be that introspective, that reflective. Would I look back and think it was magic or tragic? Holly would want me to think magic, each tragedy being overwhelmed by the magic. I thought it was a matter of willpower, the ability to move on and create new stories regardless of the tragedies. It's got to be your disposition, outlook, temperament. There was another story I wanted to tell Holly, one I was ashamed of—I guess a tragic story.

"I was still staying in the loft. The weather was turning cold in late November. The hayloft had no heating and no insulation, and the wind passed through the cracks in the floorboards. I was sleeping in my clothes, surrounded by a thin fiberfill comforter. I stayed away as much as I could, spending more time warm at school after classes and sometimes early evenings at the library in Columbus. One night I came back, and Jake had dropped off a down sleeping bag.

"At the time this all happened, I wasn't sorry, I was indignant. Why had Jake brought this woman into our lives? Wasn't I enough? Couldn't he just get his fuck on and come back alone like he'd done in the past? We'd been fine by ourselves, and I'd been content. And Jake had never hit me.

"Another night, I was reading with my head lamp when Rose climbed the stairs. Her hair was still matted in places but now tied up with the pink bandanna. Her clothes were washed, and I could see that her pants were olive green, and her long-sleeved thermal undershirt was a tan color like khaki. She had the body of an athlete and it showed through the fabric.

"She lay down next to me and said, 'I'm not here to crash your party.' She smiled, and I could tell it was a gesture she used reluctantly. Then she said, 'I don't want to be your stepmother, I'm closer to your age than I am to Jake's—I could be your sister.' Rose looked at me with that same smile and said, 'or something more.' She kissed me on the lips. I kissed her back. What happened then seemed out-of-body, like it was happening to someone else. Rose pushed me back and kept kissing me. Then her hand went under my shirt to my breasts, then down my stomach to my pants. She unbuckled my belt and then worked the button and fly. She touched me and I can remember moving my legs so that she could get closer and inside. Her mouth left my lips and followed her hand. She pulled my pants down and I could feel her tongue inside me. She looked up once and asked, 'Are you enjoying yourself?' It was my chance to say, *No*, or *Stop*, but I closed my eyes and didn't answer. She continued.

"I won't say I didn't like it, because I did. It was something I'd thought about since that first kiss with Sarah. Rose pleasured me until we heard the door of the bunker creak open and heard Rex climbing the steps to the loft. Before she left, she said, 'Don't worry, I'm a vagabond like that pilot Amelia Earhart, and one day I'll vanish without a trace.'

"That night I hardly slept. I knew how fucked-up it was, but I fantasized about what could have been and what might be. At that moment I was attracted to Rose, and I wanted the touch of another woman. And then in my mind it felt all fucked-up—Rose, Ruby, Jake. Was she first trying to be my stepmother and now trying to be my lover? In the end, I was repulsed and embarrassed and ashamed of myself for being intimate with her and having sexual thoughts. By the morning I couldn't stomach seeing either, see the looks on their faces, maybe a coy look from Rose. I left for school before the sun was up. I resolved to move out, move to the river on the other side of the forest.

"I'm comfortable with myself—Jake taught me how to be alone, hell, he forced me to be alone. I'm tough and can provide for myself under most circumstances. I spent that next week building a shack of sorts. The flotsam of the river included lumber and boards from old buildings swept away by spring floods. I found plastic tarps. I had enough wood to make the skeleton of walls and a roof, then enough plastic to keep out the wind and rain. I bought warmer clothes at the Goodwill. At a junk store I found an old two-burner gas stove and a Coleman lantern. The lantern itself would heat the shack to a tolerable state, but one day a gas catalytic heater was on my doorstep along with four gallons of white gas. I guess Jake had discovered where I was staying, and this was his way of saying he still cared. I spent the first part of the winter living in the shack, using the school locker room to clean up, then staying late at school or the library in town to do my homework. I provided for what I needed—food, water, whatever—by selling the weed that Jake now delivered directly to Cody. I made it work.

"Christmas passed but without much observance. Jake didn't believe in religion and thought Christmas was just a tool of capitalists to sell more stuff that no one needed. There was nothing I missed. I assumed Rose wasn't a Christmas person either, and I suspect there might have been bad emotional baggage left behind in Tarzana.

"I insulated the shack with more layers of plastic sheeting. I dug an outdoor toilet and hammered together a seat of sorts with a view of the river.

"The Platte never completely froze that year. In front of my shack the muddy water moved through the banks of ice like a snake under leaves. I was making about fifty dollars a week selling weed, enough to keep me in food and fuel. I cleaned my dishes in the river, showered in the girls' locker room at school, and washed my clothes at a coin-op Laundromat in town. From time to time,

Jake would leave meat or eggs or veggies in front of the shack while I was at school, but I went for two months without seeing him or Rose.

"Early February, on a Saturday, I heard heavy footsteps in the woods. Instinctively I knew it was Jake. He opened the door to the shack and told me that Rose had left.

"It was cold out, but he wasn't wearing his cap. His hair was unbound and clung to his shoulders like matted grass. He looked like he hadn't slept, and he stood there staring at me, wanting something, but I wasn't sure what.

"I asked then if he knew about Rose and me.

"Jake looked around my shack, I guess trying to figure out if he should evade or plow through with the truth. He went for evasion. He said, 'It was Rose's idea.'

"I said, 'Nothing happens in your domain that isn't your idea, that you don't initiate.' I added, 'Everything is different now, you know that?'

"Then he pulled out a letter from his back pocket, my college acceptance letter from Brown.

"I moved back to the bunker before the spring flooding reduced my shack to the flotsam it had once been. We never talked about Rose after that, and we never discussed what happened. She had, like she said, vanished without a trace. But our relationship was strained and different. The shame was there between us—that he'd fucked with my life and my sexuality in a way that breached a trust, and I could no longer trust him to do the right thing.

"I was also leaving in the fall and going to college."

33

Four caribou were in the water ahead of me swimming across the Thelon from the north shore. Swarms of gulls squawked above. One caribou had antlers three feet tall, topped by a small spread of points like thick, gloved fingers. They drifted as I drifted, and I watched. When I finally neared them, they'd reached the bank and shaken off the river water. Their hides were splotchy with molting fur. The last one out was slighter than the others, a calf or small cow. I could see its ribs outlined beneath hide, and I thought it easy prey for waiting or trailing wolves. It was then I noticed gulls picking through the clots of caribou fur that had washed up on shore, and I realized that hundreds of molting caribou must have passed across this channel before these stragglers. I kept paddling.

Toward morning a bank of dark clouds chased me from the west. In an hour they'd catch up, and the clouds would spit rain and keep the temperature cool and allow me to keep paddling into the day. The weather felt like autumn in Nebraska, and I wondered if the brief summer of the Arctic was already coming to an end. I found a camping spot marked by a cairn. On the shore I saw footprints in the sand, recently left, maybe by the Kawishiwi campers. I knew they were still days ahead, but the possibility of them slowing down and taking a day off was there, and I looked for any sign. I put my Muck Boot next to a footprint. The sizing was close and I counted the individual tracks—four girls. I compared the freshness of my print with theirs. The contours of the sand were eroded by gravity and wind, but I wanted to believe that they'd passed just hours before. The proximity was overwhelming, intoxicating, and I wanted to get back in the canoe and keep paddling. I looked for other signs. Farther down the shore I found the remains of a campfire. The charred ends of driftwood were cold. The water they'd used to extinguish the fire had evaporated and the coals were dry. I figured at least two days. Whatever excitement I had was deflated and left me with the exhaustion of lost hope. Holly was already beneath the waves, and I just needed to sleep.

I WOKE UP four hours later to rain and wind battering my tent. I sat covered and waited out the squall. I tried to think of what I could eat. I craved carbs, pasta, and—more than that—I craved meat, real meat like venison or lake trout, but the fishing gear had been lost in the accident. I was losing weight, I figured twenty pounds from my midsection and thighs. I stirred together what I felt I could stomach—brownie mix, shortening, and oatmeal.

I removed the bandage over my forehead. A thin, moist film covered the laceration and I could now leave it open to dry and scab. There was no irritation or infection.

The rain stopped and the wind abated, and I crawled from the tent. By the shore something moved. I watched and then saw the brown fur of an animal near where I'd submerged Holly. *Fuck*. I ran in my socks across the sharp stones of the beach. I screamed, just a loud keening wail that I'd never heard come from my mouth. It was the size of a small dog, and I thought a bear cub or a big raccoon. Then the animal reared on its back legs and hissed, making a stand. I recognized its long snout, short legs, gray stripes of fur running down its side, and a tail—wolverine. I charged toward it, screaming. Our confrontation became a game of chicken, who was going to flinch first. Anger in me welled up, all the rage I had for this place, for this predicament. I kept running. Then the wolverine did back down and waddled away on its short legs upriver and out of sight.

I reached the shore and saw that the sleeping bag was punctured with wet tufts of goose down streaked against the fabric and moving with the slight current of water. I pulled off the weights. Holly's body floated to the surface and I lifted her from the river. The smell of rot hit me. I carried her body and tried not to breathe. I laid her on the shore. I could see a hole that tunneled through the sleeping bag and the fabric of Holly's clothes. I saw purple-greenish shades of rotting flesh. I needed to breathe. I moved away and turned my head, but the stench of Holly's decomposing and bloated body was still with me. I stepped back and vomited onto the ground.

I held my breath and sealed up the hole with more duct tape. I wrapped more tape around the sleeping bag to cover as much of the seeping fluids and smell as possible. I placed Holly in the canoe and got back on the river to continue chasing the campers.

THE SEARING

34

On the map the Thelon Bluffs were crosshatched with the rail-road tracks of rapids. I planned to rest at the start of the bluffs and then navigate the rapids in the early evening before the half-dark of night. I pushed off with Holly in the bow. I had thirty miles to paddle before the sun rose above the tundra.

The river was as wide as the Platte with the same slow current, and I paddled three strokes each side, back and forth, to keep the canoe moving at a steady pace. My mind drifted to Holly and what our life might have been. I wanted to imagine what the two of us would be like as mothers. There was a story buried in my head somewhere and I let it unfold.

"Theo was smart from the beginning. He could speak a string of words before he could walk and could carry on a conversation before he was potty trained. We don't have a television in the house—you think it makes us intellectually lazy. You're that kind of parent, a bit judgy. You're a professor and a writer, and that whole intellectual persona drives your parenting and sometimes your relationship with me. I'm the down-to-earth type—I never had a television, so what do I know? I actually think television might heighten intellectual curiosity, but I'm not sure, nor do I have a strong enough opinion to voice it. We're all liable to be as wrong as we are right. Why judge? And I'm not the type to use the words *intellectual curiosity*. I'm just a carpenter. While you work on the kid's mind, I make him building blocks from scraps of wood. We play. And I think you and I balance each other. It's why we love each other.

"Theo grows. We send him to public school, and he tests into a gifted and talented program. You get him involved with cross-country skiing in the winter and canoeing in the summer. At age eight he starts at Camp Kawishiwi. You want him to enjoy the outdoors and canoeing, and you want him to follow in your footsteps—our footsteps—and canoe the Barrens. You have a vision for his life, and you're more opinionated about Theo's upbringing than I am. I don't disagree. I'm happy that he has a life completely different from what I lived. But some habits die hard—I love to hunt.

"I go alone because I don't trust others with guns, and I've learned to value being by myself in the woods. It's comforting and contemplative. I can think and make sense of things. I can also completely zone out and just enjoy the hunt. I drive clear up to the national forest on the Canadian border and then walk in. After a day's hike, there are no more sounds of gunshots. Most hunters stick close to the roads and their four-wheelers. Most are content with huddling in a deer stand, nipping from a flask, and waiting for twigs to snap. I like to camp for a few days and stalk. I get close to my prey and understand their movements. I move with them. I'm good at hunting and always bring back venison.

"Then, one year, Theo asks if he can join me. This is difficult for you. You don't like hunting and don't feel comfortable
with killing. Like most folks, I guess, you prefer your killing san-
itized and manufactured, just another link in the industrial food
chain. But you also know you're a hypocrite. If Theo never asked
to join me, I would have never brought it up. But he did, and I
do want to share my passions. I want to take him along, and you
say, 'Okay.'

"Theo is ten years old. He can join me but he's not old enough
to carry and shoot a rifle even though I was taking deer and other
animals at his age. We hike in and camp, and he's a real trooper,
no complaining or crying. I think he enjoys it. The next day we
stalk, and I look for the deer trails that crisscross the forest. I look
for meadows where deer might bed down. I find the high ledges
where I can glass the area, looking for a rack of antlers or movement of brush. It's Theo with my binoculars who sees the buck
first. He points, 'There!' I see the movement and the glint of light
off his antlers as he moves through the brush. I know the direction he's going, and I move with Theo across the ridge to get in
range. An hour later I have my shot and the buck goes down. My
aim is good—I think a neck shot or double lung or heart. I won't
be chasing this deer like I'd done with Jake years earlier. We move
down the ridge and find the buck. I think a double lung, there's no
breath. I pulled out my folding Buck knife, a tool Jake had given
me. I show Theo how to harvest the meat. I let him do some of the
work while I explain each step. Then I show him how to harvest
the heart and consume it in the field. That's what Jake did, and I
do. Christians eat the symbolic bread of Christ; we eat the very real
blood-pumping heart of our kill. It's acknowledging the cycles of
nature; it's the visceral acceptance of another's sacrifice.

"When we get home, Theo tells you about eating the heart. You don't know what to do with the information, and I think it disgusts you. You smile and say nothing. Then you quickly change the subject and find an excuse to leave the house. I don't see you for hours, and that night you're unusually quiet, almost frosty. I just let it go, or maybe sink in. Days later you want to speak with me. I say, 'Okay.'

"You say you're sorry. You explain what it's like to be in your head. You want Theo's life to be perfect, a pre-imagined story that follows a set of rules set forth by you, by your colleagues, by writers of newspaper and magazine stories, by society. But you don't want to be like that, like your mother with her vision of the perfect wedding. You say that I'm the antithesis, what keeps you real, why you love me, but that it's hard to accept sometimes. I explain what I think it means, having two very different parents. And what it means is that we're providing Theo with the widest range of experiences that we can afford and accommodate. It means reading Tolstoy and comic books, cross-country skiing and playing football, watching documentaries and reality TV, camping out and dining out, eating tofu and raw venison heart. Providing choices. Then Theo can find the form and stories for his own life. He can make his own choices. This makes you smile. You're happy that I can feed our son the heart of a hunted buck. You tell me again that you love me, and I'm so proud of you."

35

I'd wanted to ask Holly why she came back to the Barrens. She described the beauty, the remoteness, and I understood that. But really, *why?* Somehow, I thought it defined her, that her experience on the Thelon had colored her whole outlook on the world.

My high school adviser, Lonnie, once told me her story of growing up in a strict religious home on a remote Nebraska farm. Like me, she was an only child. Her parents were Missouri Synod Lutherans—no dances, no singing, no laughing, no prom, no dates—most of which she tolerated. But the stoicism of her parents, their silence and the overall lack of personal contact with others, bothered Lonnie—the isolation they enforced—which I completely understood. After graduating from high school, she joined a church mission to Brazil. She stayed in a small home that sheltered an extended family that included parents, a grandparent, the father's sister, and five children. Lonnie described the excitement in the house with so many people interacting—the energy, the bickering, and the love. The absorption of it all filled her like never before, and that feeling was Lonnie's epiphany.

Lonnie knew then that what she wanted was the happiness of a full house and a big, raucous family. Her missionary experience had defined her; she went on to have four children and a home filled with noise and love. Maybe Holly learned in the Barrens that what she wanted was more adventure, more unique experiences, and more stories to tell. Maybe she needed to see the Barrens again to reengage or reaffirm the person she'd discovered she was. I thought then that maybe my life would be defined by my journey with Holly down the Thelon and through the Barrens.

THE BLUFFS WERE a change in the landscape, a break in the monotony of endless flat tundra. They lined the river on both sides, rising a hundred feet to an overlooking plateau. Ahead, I saw ripples of water, what looked like a manageable set of rapids that moved gradually to a bend in the river. I paddled on, using strokes to keep to the deep water. At the bend I heard the deeper roar of more dangerous rapids, and then I saw the horizon of water disappear over a ledge. I couldn't tell the height of the ledge, so I steered to the shore and pulled up to scout ahead. The cryptic note Holly had written on the map said simply, "Depends."

The drop was three feet with water spilling into a hole that could trap and swamp a canoe. Beyond that was a torrent of whitewater through countless obstacles with no navigable route that I could see. And I thought, *Depends on what?* Two weeks ago, I thought Holly and I would've lined this stretch, guiding the canoe over the ledge and through the rocks from shore. The Kawishiwi campers had probably lined this stretch. I had to portage and consequently was going to lose time.

I carried Holly across first. I was stronger than I'd been weeks ago. I could feel the strength in my arms and shoulders, and lifting

Holly was not as hard as it was back at the Canyon. Her body lay across my shoulder and against my neck. The smell of rotting flesh was there, just noticeable but not overwhelming. Maybe I'd become used to it.

Cresting a hill, I saw ten musk ox in the distance grazing on Arctic shrubs. I knew that when threatened, the musk ox would form a defensive circle around their calves. But as I passed within fifty feet, they made no motion, not one looked up to acknowledge my presence. Past the rapids I laid Holly in slack water and tied the tether to rocks. The portage was a half-mile and took four trips. Each time I passed the musk ox, they continued their grazing and, like the caribou days before, ignored my presence. I wasn't a predator, not a toxic threat—I wasn't there to fuck up their lives. Maybe I was just another animal scurrying at their periphery, or part of the landscape like a rock or tree. Whatever I was, I knew I belonged.

I made the final trip with the canoe, reloaded everything, and got back on the Thelon.

The bluff walls narrowed, funneling the river into a swift and deep current. I ruddered to keep straight to the channel and looked ahead for the whitecaps of rapids that I instinctively knew would be there. Again, I heard the rapids before I saw them and pulled off to scout. Holly had made no notes on the map, and no cairns marked a portage, so it was likely that the rapids were easily passable.

I followed a caribou trail that zigzagged up through a ravine cut in the bluffs. At the top I could see the whitewater as it moved within a tight gorge. I was frightened of the edge, scared of falling, and crawled cautiously near to scout. The river flowed in a bend around the bluff, around me. The water closest moved through a garden of rocks that was impassable, but the other side was unobstructed, a flume of water without a ripple of white. Below the flume was a short drop into a standing wave, easy if I hit it straight. I felt confident I could navigate this set of rapids, and I'd already lost time on the portage. I needed to catch up.

I walked back down from the bluff and pushed off in the canoe. I used my strategy—slow down, back-paddle, and look for the deep water at the outside of the bend. I got closer and the river surged up with a hand that pushed me forward and took me with it toward the flume. I paddled on my strong side, my left hand on the handle, the blade on the right side of the canoe. The water propelled me in its own direction, and now I switched sides continually to keep my bow pointed downriver. On my right I passed the rock garden and crashing water that threw up spray. My eyes blinked and my head shook to clear my vision. I gulped air and kept paddling, then rudder-steering through the bend. It was then I saw a submerged boulder I hadn't seen from the bluff, a shadow just beneath the surface. The hand of the river gave me little choice to slow down or change course.

The rock hit the canoe below the bow and near Holly, the noise like a rifle shot. Water spilled through a fresh crack in the hull. The canoe bounced to the left and then the river pushed us sideways, threatening to dump me downstream. I leaned into the roll of the canoe and ruddered hard to move the bow back downriver. And for a second, I had it, my full body into the roll, my bow inching to the right. Water spilled through the hull but controlled like the spigot of a drinking fountain. I just needed to get to shallow water.

Then the hand of the river pushed me up again and the canoe was overcome and swamped by a wall of pent-up water that gushed over the gunwale. I was thrown into the icy water along with both packs. Holly's body, tethered and held in by the front thwart, stayed secured. I held on to the stern as I was dragged behind. The canoe moved through the final turbulence of the rapids, pulling at my arm. Then I lost my grip. The hand of the water pushed my body where it wanted. My arms flailed to slow my descent, my feet kicked to find river bottom, and I waited for a rock to bash my head. The life vest kept my head up, and I found room to breathe. Then a sweep of water thrust me over the last ledge and into a hole. My body was pushed back under and I was stuck there by the force of the water, tumbling like Holly had tumbled in the canyon. I was under for what felt like minutes. I willed myself to hold air in my lungs. My hand found the ledge, then my foot, and I pushed up, and then I was out and through the standing wave. I bobbed to the calm surface and sucked air. My breathing was shallow, my heart racing.

I swam to the swamped canoe and guided it to the closest shore. I was cold but not hurt, but my hands were numb and I was shivering. I kicked off my Muck Boots and swam out into deeper water to where the P-pack with the weights had sunk. I could see it beneath the water, a dark spot against the sand bottom. I dove down to retrieve the pack and dragged it back to the canoe. My paddle and the food pack had washed up on the opposite bank, and I swam for those.

I still shivered from the wet and cold. There was no wood for a fire, but the sun was rising and warming the air and rocks. I pulled out everything wet and set up the tent. I kept moving and let my clothes dry against my skin. I checked the canoe hull and found the breach, an opened crack about three inches long that I'd need to somehow repair.

The wrapped sleeping bag with Holly inside rested on the sand near the canoe, and I sat down beside her. I'd calmed and now weariness overwhelmed me like a warm blanket. I wanted to find sleep and peace, but I just sat there alone, lonely without Holly. I felt a yearning to open the sleeping bag and hold her hand. I wanted to talk with her again and tell her something. But what? I wanted to say what it was I thought I'd discovered, how the Barrens would define me. But it wasn't something I knew right then, and it wasn't something I could consciously decide. It would just become, and I'd know it when I could look back and see the changes, the patterns, the choices I made. What I did know was that the river itself would define me in some way. The Thelon and maybe the Platte, and that I would always need to be near a river.

36

When I woke, I checked on the canoe. The water had drained through the crack in the hull, and it took me a moment to think what Jake would do, what I should do. A thick inch of duct tape was still on the roll, the tape two inches wide with a waterproof coating. I lined the hull inside and out with tape. I laid the canoe in the river, loaded the packs, and looked for leaks. The repair seemed tight.

By dusk I was on the Thelon again and moving past the Bluffs. Soon I would cross from map 66D to 66C, Beverly Lake. I planned to camp at Beverly Lake near a high overlook where I desperately hoped to see the canoes or the campfire of the Kawishiwi group.

I took a paddle stroke, then switched sides. I kept talking to Holly.

"In my senior year, Cody and I still shared our weed business. Throughout that winter I wore tall rubber boots with two pairs of socks. The tops went almost to my knees, and that's where I carried the weed in quarter-ounce baggies. I figured that if caught, or ripped off, they'd go for my locker or backpack but not the boots. And there I was wrong.

"One Friday in February the school administrator, a mousy woman who worked the front desk and collected students' sick and tardy notes, came into my social studies class and asked me to go to the principal's office. I picked up my heavy backpack and followed. Inside the office were two cops, a man and woman. They explained that they'd had a complaint about drug dealing at Columbus High and I was singled out.

"They searched my backpack first and found nothing. Then I was escorted down the hall to my locker. I opened the door, and they searched through my stuff—just books, school supplies, and some dirty laundry. Then it was back to the principal's office. The woman cop's name tag said simply, "Forest." She said she needed to search me and to stand with my hands above my head. She did her search from top to bottom and found my stash of weed almost instantly. I was cuffed and walked past a line of kids who'd just been let out of class. I walked with my head down, unable to look into the eyes of any student. Forest opened the back door of the squad car and rested her hand on top of my head to guide me in. She pushed the seat belt across my lap and chest, my hands painfully clasped behind me.

"At the police station I was booked—photographed, finger-printed, and asked my name, birth date, address, parents' names. It was Forest who interviewed me later. I remember seeing the top of a neck tattoo poking above her tight collar—bad girl gone straight. Tough girl. Then she explained—I had more than an ounce of marijuana, which constituted possession with intent to distribute. That alone was only a misdemeanor, a hundred-dollar fine and a few days in the county jail. But Forest explained that with a charge of selling drugs to a minor within a thousand feet of a school—or in a school—I was looking at a felony. I was seventeen and could be charged as an adult. I was looking at one to fifty years in the state prison. Then the questions: Who had I sold to? Who had I bought from? Who else was dealing drugs at Columbus High? I said nothing and just stared at my hands. I wasn't ready to talk about the stupidity of what I'd done or who I'd done it with—and Forest could go fuck herself. Then I was taken to a holding cell. On the way, we passed back through the booking room, and there was Cody on a bench looking up at me, worried. I thought then that I would be going to jail and not finishing high school. I had gotten into college and been awarded a full scholarship. That was all gone.

"That evening I was taken the one block down Main Street to the court house and led to a cell in the old jail on the second floor. I was told there would be a bail hearing the next day and that I would meet my court-appointed lawyer.

"I was anxious, frightened. It was stupid to be selling weed at school. I should have known that sooner or later some kid was going to rat me out or tell their parents when caught with a joint. It was as if my life was all shit, I was shit, and this was my true form, my real destiny. I deserved it, and maybe I wanted it—starting off my adult life in prison. I was offered a call, but I had no one I wanted to talk with.

"The next day my assigned public defender spoke to me through the bars for all of fifteen minutes. His name was Douglas Ernst—Doug. He looked maybe thirty, short, and already sprouting a beer gut. His suit hung off his sloping shoulders with sleeves that almost covered his knuckles. He had that goatee fashionable among anyone in Nebraska who drove a pickup, shot birds, or watched tractor pulls, which covered just about everyone. I had been charged with a Class 2 felony, distribution within a thousand feet of a school. He did not ask me if I was innocent or guilty, and I'm sure he assumed my guilt. He said I'd be in front of the judge later that day to determine bail. A Class 2 felony ranked me up there with robbery, human trafficking, assault with a deadly weapon, and rape. Based on state guidelines, Doug explained, bail could be as high as twenty-five thousand. I told him then that I'd done what they said, I had dealt drugs to my classmates. He said nothing.

"I sat in the courtroom, waiting for my name to be called. I listened to the judge and listened as Doug handled other cases—DUIs, possession, assault, breaking and entering. I never imagined all this went on in Columbus with its population of twenty thousand. Most were released without having to post bail. I stood when my name was called. Then Doug was in front of the judge again. The county prosecutor read my charges and explained the severity of the crime and asked for bail to be set at thirty thousand dollars. Doug explained to the judge that this was my first offense and that I was a lifelong resident of Columbus. My bail hearing lasted all of five minutes with bail set at twenty thousand. I had no way to make bail, nor would Jake, nor would I ask him. The next day I was transported an hour north of town to the juvenile detention center. I was issued an orange jumpsuit and assigned a cell that, for the rest of my stay, I shared with a girl my age. She'd stabbed her boyfriend and cried most of the time.

"Three days later I had a visit from Doug. We talked in a conference room. He seemed more relaxed outside the courthouse and took his time explaining the situation. He'd gone to the school and spoke with the principal. A parent had found marijuana on their daughter, the daughter had told where she purchased the weed, and the parent had complained. The daughter would testify if needed, and Doug was sure the prosecutor could find other witnesses if it came to that. Doug had talked to my adviser, Lonnie. He knew about my acceptance to college and the scholarship. Doug wanted me to go to college. Doug had seen my records at Child Protection Services from when Jake had kept me out of school. Then he talked to Jake. I was wrong about Doug—I'd made a dumb assumption based merely on his appearance. He did care.

"Doug had seen where I lived and how I lived. He didn't say much about what he saw, and I assumed he thought I was mistreated somehow. He knew Jake had supplied the marijuana that I sold. He'd confronted Jake and told him the consequences I was facing. The next day Jake turned himself in. Jake confessed that he'd grown the marijuana, that he coerced Cody and me into selling the drugs to kids at the high school. Jake made his confession to the district attorney in exchange for our release. Child Services allowed me to be released into the custody of my adviser, Lonnie. She was outside the courthouse, waiting to take me to her home. She didn't ask for details, didn't lecture. Lonnie just said, 'Let's go home.'

"I didn't realize it then, but my life with Jake had come to an end. At the time I didn't blame Jake for what had happened, but I should have. His arrogance had displaced his judgment. He should have been more careful with my life, his life, and the life we shared. I knew then that I needed to take control of my life, to start making my own decisions. I would never again let him or anyone else tell me to shut the fuck up."

37

Hours from the Bluffs the river turned north and spread across a valley with a long, half-mile-wide island separating two channels. I stopped at the tip of the island and checked the map. Holly hadn't written notes, and both channels emptied into Beverly Lake. I chose the east side, thinking it the shorter route. An hour later the channel dispersed into hundreds of sandbars. I tried to keep to the deep water, but then it trickled out and I was compelled to pull the canoe with its heavy load across the narrow sweeps of sand. I knew the campers wouldn't have made the mistake of taking this route, and I was losing more time.

I looped the climbing rope around my shoulder and hip and pulled like a harnessed animal. My progress was slow. Blowflies that I hadn't seen before swarmed to the smell of Holly's wrapped body. I crossed a long stretch of sand, pulling the three hundred pounds of gear loaded in the seventy-pound canoe like a sled on snow. I crossed shallow water and then more sand and for hours kept pulling. The exhaustion hit me all at once, and I stumbled and fell with my shoulder buried in sand. I curled into myself and cried for what seemed an eternity. It was everything, the over-whelming exhaustion, my life, the river journey, what I would face when, *if,* I got back to civilization—the loss of Holly, the state of her body. The emotions surrounding that self-pity all drained through my tears until they dried and I knew I needed to get up and keep moving. I finally stood and started hauling again. It was another hour before I found deep water where I could resume paddling.

Ahead I could see a rocky point maybe forty feet high. I thought that if I could make the point, I'd camp for the day and start across Beverly in the evening. I could climb the point and look across the lake for any sign of the Kawishiwi campers.

I reached the point by the time the sun was at its zenith. I was dead tired but climbed regardless—I had to see if the women were on the lake and within sight. On top was a firepit with the rem-nants of wood recently burned. Maybe they'd camped here. The coals were still moist from being doused—they might have been here yesterday. The lake was ten miles long and four or five miles wide, a vast expanse of water that I'd not seen since Eyeberry Lake weeks earlier. I scanned for any sight of canoes or paddles cutting through the air. Nothing moved above the expanse of water. I wished we'd brought binoculars.

I camped on the top, tying down the tent with the rocks that were scattered everywhere and had probably been used for the same purpose. The surrounding land was bare, and I didn't have driftwood for a fire. I craved fresh protein, real meat, but all I had was TVP, powdered eggs, and oatmeal. I wanted carbs, I wanted fat, pork fat, but all I had was shortening. I put together a mush of ingredients and waited until the TVP was somewhat hydrated. I choked it down before falling asleep. I dreamt of food.

By the time I woke, the wind had picked up from the east and the sky was dark with ominous gray clouds. I felt the beginnings of a headache. I crawled from my sleeping bag and stepped from the tent to look out again across the lake. Then I saw it, a thin line of smoke rising from an island maybe five miles in the distance—the campers. Renewed energy pulsed through my body with the thought that the campers were real, that I could possibly reach them within a day. I knew then that what I'd been chasing was not a mere apparition or false hope.

I packed up quickly and walked down to the canoe. At the shoreline I saw the waves crashing up and sending a spray of cold water into the air. The waves pushed by the east wind had built to three feet and there was no way I could paddle against them. I screamed for help as loud as I could, but I knew they couldn't hear me across the miles of lake and above the roar of the wind. My optimism turned to dread, then anger—fuck! Nothing to do but wait and hope that the Kawishiwi campers were also windbound. I checked the map. Past the island, the path to Aberdeen Lake went south through a maze of channels and islands protected from the wind. They might be able to get there—I might not.

38

The gusting east wind pulled in cold air, and the clouds became dark and low. The bugs were grounded so I exchanged my bug shirt for a down jacket I found in Holly's P-pack. I walked the shoreline and hunted for driftwood. Three hours later I had an armload and hiked up the point and started a fire. I kept the wind to my back, the smoke of the fire billowing away to the west, and I wondered if the campers could see the smoke. I could see theirs.

I had time now and pulled out the frying pan that hadn't been used since the canyon. I added water to the pancake mix. I balanced the pan on rocks and heated shortening, then added the batter. The pancake puffed up in the heat, and I flipped the cake when the edges turned dark brown. I scooped brown sugar on top and ate the entire cake, then made another. Afterward, I told my last story about Jake.

"I visited the bunker once after I started living with Lonnie. It was late spring, a four-day weekend in mid-April. Senior classes were winding down, trees had leafed out—a beautiful day—and I just took off walking. Lonnie lived on a farm south of the Platte near a village called Octavia, really just a cluster of houses, a post office, and an auto junkyard. I walked the mile to Octavia, then put out my thumb. The news of the arrests had been in the paper, and people out in the country probably knew who I was or had an inkling. I didn't get a ride. I walked five more miles to the highway and then was able to get a ride from a stranger. I walked the last mile down our gravel road. The bunker hadn't changed, but the door was open and I could see an egress window that had been smashed. I took the steps down and walked in. The place had been trashed and looted. Our guns were gone; food had been pulled from the shelves and littered the floor. Clothes were everywhere, and they'd found Jake's stash of dollars hidden in the cavity of the duck decoy. I looked for anything that might bring me back, any remnant of my life with Jake that I could take with me. What I found was the Buck knife that Jake had given me before I could shoot a gun. Outside, the yard was empty, the chickens and goats gone.

"I had some good memories, the oldest from when I was three. Jake was trying to teach me the ABCs, but I wasn't catching on—I just couldn't remember all twenty-six letters. Then he sang the rhyme. It was maybe the only time I remember Jake singing, and I picked up on the letters right away. Then I made him sing me that song each night. I'd shout, 'One more time, one more time,' until he sang, and then he'd sing it until I finally fell asleep.

"Then there were the bad memories—Rose, Forest, Sarah, Jericho, Jake.

"In the barn I found cans of white gas we'd used for the lanterns and my catalytic heater. I took one inside the bunker. I built a burn pile of busted furniture and books. I doused the pile with gas and lit it up. I took another can and started a fire in the barn and then the chicken coop. The flames consumed everything. I watched from the woods as fire trucks came and the firemen contained the fire to the property. By early evening they were gone.

"I sat on a stump that Jake had used to split wood. This was what remained of my childhood, a burnt hole in the ground. I wanted to remember the good things—the ABCs, living close to my father, exploring the woods, hunting, cooking, growing, learning—each tragedy overwhelmed by the magic. But I'd always known I was an aberration, that Jake was an aberration. For me to move on, Jake, the bunker, Columbus, needed to be behind me. Dead, a burnt hole in the ground.

"The following August, Lonnie drove me east to Providence. We passed the prison in Lincoln where Jake was doing his time. I'd thought about Jake since the arrest. I realized that his idea of living outside of society included poaching animals—including his neighbor's—taking the government's handouts, and selling drugs to kids. I almost never left Nebraska, never went to college, and almost never met you.

"Lonnie asked if I wanted to stop. I said, 'No.'"

SNOW WAS FALLING in horizontal gusts when I crawled into the tent, the wind still blasting from the east. It was hard for me to sleep with my body now accustomed to paddling nights. I finally did fall asleep and slept well into the morning. I woke startled—I'd lost paddling time. But the wind still howled, and I knew I was still trapped. I lay back in the sleeping bag and just listened to the wind.

Hours later I broke down the tent and packed the sleeping bag, ready for when the wind subsided and the waves diminished. My driftwood was gone and I ate oatmeal soaked in cold water.

Afterward, I went down to check on Holly. I could see the silver duct tape wrapping on the sleeping bag beneath the waves, the end of the tether reaching toward the surface and moving with the rocking water.

I walked along the shore and then headed inland. Near a stand of spruce on a rock outcropping I could see the lake and the island where the campers were. I thought I saw the red of canoes on the shore but wasn't sure. I kept walking inland. In the distance was another rise, and I walked to the top. On the other side stood a herd of caribou, maybe fifty or more grazing in a meadow of shrubs and lichens. Nearby was a rock pile, larger than a cairn, human-made. It looked to be a primitive hunter's blind of some sort. I walked to the blind from the west, knowing the caribou wouldn't be able to scent me. I leaned against the rocks of the blind and watched.

I saw just-born calves with their mothers. One larger animal was on the edge of the herd with antlers that climbed double its height. Five points spread out from the top palm like the outstretched hands of some mythical giant. The antlers of the lower bez looked like two hands in prayer. I was awed. It looked in my direction and then walked toward me, and the others followed. All passed by the blind as I lay tucked close to the rocks. I saw their broad hooves covered in hair, almost cartoonish in their size. One calf sniffed at Holly's down jacket. All around me were legs and hooves—close enough to touch, close enough to be trampled, but none touched me. Then they were gone.

I climbed back up the rise to the stand of spruce. I headed northeast and reached another rise. Below was the lake and the island not two miles away, and now I saw two canoes being pulled into the water. Sun reflected off the movement of paddles. The canoes headed from the lee of the island to the open water. I watched them cross with their bows angled into the oncoming waves. They moved into the channel that led to Aberdeen Lake. I ran back to my campsite.

Hours later the wind finally abated. I paddled out toward the island and then through the channel toward Aberdeen Lake. A headwind slowed my progress. I knew I was losing ground to the campers. But if they paddled eight hours, I could paddle twelve, so I kept going. I checked the map every few miles, the compass lined up to the contours of the land.

I passed a lone bull moose. He looked up from his stand of willows and then moved slowly away from the shore. A flock of gulls circled above a rock reef and squawked. I hadn't seen gulls in days, and now I wondered if they might be a sign of civilization, like Columbus seeing his white bird and following it to land. It was a funny idea that occupied my mind while more time passed. But then the thought of civilization brought me back to the inevitable confrontation with people, authorities, parents. And for the next hour I tried to verbalize in my head what had happened, how it happened, why the two of us were paddling in the Barrens. And then I told the story out loud to myself, the way Holly would've wanted me to tell it—her life before she fell, her fall, and then my journey to get Holly back to her family.

I followed the channel that jogged north for a few miles then east. I kept going. The sun peeked intermittently through the breaking clouds as it made its way across and around the horizon, circling back to the north. I passed a small island, just a wind-carved mound of white sand that looked like the curve of Holly's back and shoulders. The channel widened, and I saw the vast expanse of water that was Aberdeen Lake. My map ended where the lake began. Another map encompassed just Aberdeen, fifty miles across.

I pulled off at a spit of land that sloped to a twenty-foot peak and hiked up to look for the campers. Nothing—no smoke or any spot of color that could be a tent or canoe. The campers could be hidden anywhere among the hundreds of inlets and islands.

39

I woke in the middle of the Arctic night to the wind ripping at the tent. The windward edge wanted to lift up, so I rolled over in the sleeping bag to hold it down. I worried about the weather and my chances of paddling the next morning. I imagined the waves building up along the massive expanse of water. I tried to think through what I could do—cover the bow of the canoe with the tent canopy and paddle through the waves, stay close to the shore and walk with the canoe, maybe strike out on foot and hope I reached the campsite of the canoers—but I wouldn't leave Holly.

I couldn't fall back asleep. I finally slid the sleeping bag off my body and legs. The Carhartt pants next to me were worn thin and stank, and I was cold. I found a pair of Holly's windproof paddling pants and a pair of long underwear. In Yellowknife these clothes would never have fit, but now I slipped them on easily. I was losing weight and needed to eat, but I couldn't eat until I saw the lake and the waves. I opened the tent flap and stepped out.

My campsite was up high, and already I could see the white-caps out on the lake. I walked down to the shore and watched the waves pile up and push water almost to the canoe. I realized there would be no paddling today and pulled the canoe farther away from the threatening waves. My only consolation was that the Kawishiwi campers were likely also windbound.

There was no driftwood on the bare spit of land to make a fire and cook, so I forced down a soupy mix of powdered eggs and pan-cake mix. Later, I pulled out Holly's pack guitar. I played around with the three chords I knew and tried to find others. I tried a song Holly taught me, the Indigo Girls' "Galileo." I remembered the lyrics and stumbled through the chords. I sang, "And now I'm serving time for mistakes made by another in another lifetime." I kept singing, but in a mournful tone because that was how I felt. Another life ago, atonement.

I checked on Holly at the shoreline. Her submerged body came in and out of focus as it rose and fell with the swelling water. Back in the tent, I undressed and crawled into the sleeping bag. I stared at the red nylon roof and imagined more of the story about Holly and me in the future, maybe the last story. Once I had all the pieces, I said it out loud.

"Theo is a grown man. He went east for college just as we had done. He studied literature and philosophy, then moved to New York where you used your connections in the publishing world to help him get a job. He became an editor, and at the age of thirty married a writer whose work he edited. Her name was Maya. Then the two of them did something unexpected and wonderful—they moved back to Minneapolis. She could write anywhere, and he set up his own literary agency. Theo had a perfect eye for finding the newest voices and stories that struck a nerve with both readers and critics. You sent talent his way. They bought a craftsman bungalow, and I built furniture for their first child, a girl named Leah. Our first granddaughter, and our three names sounded just right with the combination of *l*s—Holly, Lee, and Leah—like branches of the same tree. They had another child, a boy this time, named Leif. We were great babysitters, grandmothers, then friends. Those kids pushed us along as we grew old.

"One night while in bed, I find it, a lump on your breast the size of a lima bean.

"You're brave like you've always been brave. Where I tend to bury my head in the sand, not think about what's to come, you take cancer head-on. Double mastectomy, chemotherapy, radiation, and the aftermath. It's the hardest time in our lives—the threat of death, the guilt of bad genes that could pass to Leah, the emotion of imbalanced hormones. You're brave but sometimes you just need to yell, then talk, then cry. The cancer retreats from your body and you recover. It's a second chance at life for all of us, and we waste no time.

"Both of us want to see the Barrens again. The grandchildren are older now, and both have enrolled as campers at Kawishiwi. Theo had gone to Kawi, and all of us together had paddled through the Boundary Waters. We arrange for a family trip to the Thelon. This time we have a sat phone along with a PLB. We're flown in to the confluence of the Hanbury River and the beginning of the Oasis. For three weeks it's just us, and we see no one else. Both Theo and his son, Leif, are great fishermen, and we eat lake trout or grayling almost every evening. Leah paints watercolors that use swatches of vibrant color but are also exacting in detail. We have one encounter with a grizzly that won't leave our campsite. I'm the one who unloads a can of bear spray in its snout.

We see small herds of musk ox throughout the Oasis and on the Barrens past Hornby's Point. We witness the caribou migration just before we're picked up on Beverly Lake. Maya writes a children's book about the trip that Leah illustrates. When we're home, all of us decide to build a family compound of sorts near the Boundary Waters, and each summer, we spend weeks together, canoeing, fishing, hunting, reading, eating. We call the place True North. You and I grow old.

"The cancer reappears as a spot on your lungs—you've been coughing for weeks. The doctors want to remove one lung, then do radiation followed by chemotherapy. I want you to do the treatments—you're brave, you've battled cancer before. I want to be with you always, and I want to be the first to go because I can't imagine living without you. But I can see in your eyes that you're not up for the battle. Life has been good; life has been lucky. You say to me that you're happy but that you're also tired. And it's okay, you say, death is life and it's okay, welcoming. It's your decision and we cry together and then cry some more.

"We have a few good months over the summer. Theo, Maya, Leah, and Leif are with us at True North. You don't want to travel or see anything else in this world, just your family. On Memorial Day we have roasted lamb with a risotto of wild morels from the forest. On the Fourth of July we eat fried walleye with roasted ears of corn. On Labor Day we cook a beef stew with onions and carrots and lots of red wine.

"You don't let the disease have its way. You say your goodbyes to friends over lunches and cocktails, the obvious never said but understood, and they do their crying privately to spare you the exhaustion of emotion. I'm there with you when you decide to end it, a handful of pills while resting in our bed. The following summer we spread your ashes on the lake at True North. It's what you wanted. I'm alone now."

THE STORY WAS sad, cathartic, and I mourned and cried again for the loss of her.

40

I slept for a few hours, then woke to the sound of the wind buffeting the tent. I lay for a few more hours dozing. I thought it was day twenty-six, August 5th—maybe. I finally got up, dressed, and went outside. The weather was still cold enough for snow, but the low gray clouds had moved on, leaving the wind and wisps of cirrus clouds. I looked for any sign of campers. None. I could see a higher ridge a mile down the shoreline, just visible past an esker, and walked toward it, hoping for a better lookout. Across the esker, caribou trails led in a hundred different directions. The tracks seemed old, even ancient. On the other side was a stand of black spruce, just a few stunted trees among the shrubs and lichen. On the ground near the trees were tufts of caribou fur, I thought the remnants of a wolf kill. A few yards farther on was another tuft, but nothing else—no antlers, bones, stains of blood, nothing. Little remained of the dead out here, and I wondered if the herd had witnessed the killing or somehow sensed the absence of the caribou that had gone missing. I thought about Holly and her parents, her friends. If they had no body to see, then there was no sure death, and if there existed the lingering possibility of life, then the ambiguity of what-ifs could haunt them for a lifetime. I hoped that bringing Holly back would be some consolation to those who loved her.

I crested the ridge and looked out over Aberdeen Lake. Nothing. I walked back to my camp and checked on Holly. I sat on the shoreline and waited. I was out of stories. I sat and waited for hours. I had no energy to move or eat. Later, I walked back into the tent and crawled into the sleeping bag. I waited and listened to the wind. Then I fell asleep.

I woke to silence, and it took me a minute to understand. The wind had died. I packed up quickly. I pulled Holly from beneath the lake and laid her into the canoe. I paddled out past the spit of land. I knew it was safer to stay close to shore, but the quickest way to the next bend in the lake was across the middle, so I went for it. I matched the point of the bow with the bend in the lake. I focused on the paddle blade and the whirlpools of water made by each stroke. My arms were strong, and I knew I could keep this pace forever. By midmorning I was at the bend and facing a line of islands. I pulled up to one and checked the map. Past the island was another stretch across the middle of the lake, then a channel that went south to the second, larger arm of Aberdeen. The channel was eight to ten miles away, four or five hours in the middle of the lake and miles from either shore. If I swamped, I'd die.

The wind picked up from the west, and now I had a tailwind to give me a push. With the increased speed, I made the channel in just over three hours and stopped on a small island close to shore. It was then I heard an engine. It was a strange sound after weeks of hearing nothing but the sounds of animals, birds, wind, and water. The sound didn't belong in that place, and it startled me. It got louder and I knew it was a boat, and I knew it was coming off the west arm of the lake, rounding the corner and heading into the channel. And then it appeared, a fishing boat painted camouflage green. A man was at the tiller, and a boy sat near the bow. I jumped, waved my arms, shouted. They were close and saw me right away. The man pushed the tiller away from him, and the boat headed toward the island. At the last moment the man killed the engine and pulled up the prop. The bow plowed into the beach, and the kid jumped out. I didn't know what to do, what to say, and I just stood there. I sobbed, and my entire body quivered with each sob, each suck of air. The boy stood and looked at me but didn't say anything. The man stayed seated in the stern.

Minutes passed with just the sound of my sobs. I finally found composure deep inside me and got out the consonants and vowels that made words.

"I need help."

It was the boy who talked, "Yes?"

"My friend is dead, and I need help."

The boy turned to the older man, maybe his father. He spoke in a Native language, and the man nodded his head. His skin was dark and lined with creases. He wore a baseball cap with a Blue Jays logo and bristles of short gray hair covered the tops of his ears.

He looked toward me. "Baker Lake is two days."

"Yes, Baker Lake. Thank you, thank you."

The old man moved to the bow of the boat and then stepped out onto the sand. I motioned for them to follow me to the canoe. I showed them Holly in the sleeping bag wrapped with duct tape, and they looked at her and spoke in their language. The boy told me to leave her in the canoe but load the heavy packs into the fishing boat. They helped me move the food pack and the P-pack. Inside the boat was a tarpaulin covering two dead caribou, their antlers sticking out above the gunwales. The man tied a rope to the stern of the boat, then handed the other end to the kid who tied it to the bow of the canoe. I stepped in and forced myself to hold back the sobs that again threatened to burst from my chest. I forced myself to say words that would feign some sense of composure. I told them that my name was Lee. The older man said his name was Mosa, the younger one was Peter. I took a seat in the bow next to Peter, and we left the island and followed the northern shore east. The red canoe called Quest followed thirty feet behind, its bow up and riding between the wakes. Mosa kept the outboard engine at half-throttle. There was no talking over the sound. Aberdeen Lake spread out to the south as far as I could see, the opposite shore blurred into the gray of the lake's surface.

We crossed the lake in two hours, which would have taken more than twelve to paddle. Mosa steered north through a mile-wide channel. Another hour later he stopped on an island and filled the gas tank from one of the five-gallon cans lined against the transom. We stepped out. I was more composed now, though the reality of help finding me was still settling in and my mind was spinning with thoughts of what would happen next. I stood next to Peter. He talked without pausing for any response, maybe trying to calm me in his own way with the sound of chatter. He spoke about himself—high school, hunting, sports—ordinary things that helped me find some sense of what might be normal. Mosa stayed mostly quiet, and I knew he wouldn't ask about Holly's death. But I also knew that he'd let Peter, and Peter finally did. His chatter stopped abruptly, and he just said it, "How did she die?" I knew it was the first of countless times I'd be asked that question, and I had to answer. I wasn't going to say that I couldn't talk about it, like hiding behind some wall of incomprehensible reality, like they wouldn't understand, because everyone understands death and most understand tragedy. And these two Inuit out on Aberdeen Lake in the middle of nowhere, in an almost uninhabitable landscape and climate, surely knew both. So, I gave my first answer to the inevitable question.

"She slipped and fell into the rapids at Thelon Canyon."

A simple answer that didn't allow for much cross-examination. Everyone slips, rapids are dangerous, and people die. Of course, it didn't come close to the whole story, the story I'd need to have for authorities, for Holly's family, for myself—the one I'd rehearsed in my mind for days.

We kept going. A half hour later I saw the two canoes of the Kawishiwi campers. I shouted and pointed. Mosa turned the bow toward the canoers and eased off the throttle.

PART THREE

THE MISHIPESHU

41

Mosa pulled up alongside the four girls paddling two canoes. They smiled when they saw us. Probably like me they hadn't seen another soul for weeks. I said that I'd had an accident, that the other girl I was with had died. One girl that looked my age, maybe the counselor, said they had a sat phone and that she could call for an evacuation. We were close to the north shore and all agreed to pull up on the nearest beach. The girl pointed, and Mosa throttled the engine.

Mosa powered the fishing boat up to the beach, cut the engine, and Peter jumped off. Mosa untied the canoe with Holly and handed me the rope end. I crossed the bow and jumped off into shallow water. I pulled the canoe up to the shore. The campers were still on the lake and paddling toward us. I told Peter they could go, that the canoers had a satellite phone and would call for help, but they waited nonetheless. I felt like I should've said more but my mouth felt unconnected—I thought of words, my mouth moved to form a sound, but what I wanted to say seemed meaningless or stilted. So, I kept silent, and I could sense Mosa and Peter were okay with silence. And what could they say? What could they ask?

When the campers reached the shore, Mosa pulled the starter rope on the engine and backed away from the beach. He pushed the tiller and the two left across the lake without looking back.

The girls arrived, and they pulled the bows of their canoes up onto the beach. The counselor came to me and said her name, Anne. She had wiry blond hair pulled back in a ponytail. Her face was broad and her eyes blue. She looked stocky and strong. Three other girls clustered around and introduced themselves. One was small and compact, calling herself Bean—five-foot-tall and maybe ninety pounds, just heavier than a food pack. Another was Charlotte. She was slender with straight blond hair and straight white teeth. She and Bean didn't look big enough to carry a canoe, but Holly hadn't looked big enough either. The fourth, Max, had short red hair, puffy cheeks, freckles, and thick, black-framed glasses taped together at one temple. She was the one who gazed toward my red canoe, toward Holly, and looked saddened. She touched my hand.

"I'm so sorry."

Anne lifted the flap on one of their P-packs and searched for the sat phone. She pulled out the black plastic waterproof case. The handset had an antenna that flipped up and Anne made the call. When she reached someone, she turned away so that I couldn't hear. She talked for a minute, then turned back and asked my full name. Lee Harvey. Anne looked at me like maybe I was being funny or sarcastic, giving the name of the JFK assassin. She paused for a second, smiled, then went back and finished her conversation.

She said that the camp director at Kawishiwi would call the Mountie office in Baker Lake. We should get a call back in an hour or so. Anne said we should make camp.

I pulled the packs from the canoe and carried them up the shoreline to where the scrabble of rock met the shrubs of the tundra. I pulled the canoe farther up on the shore so that I could reach for Holly. I'd done this for weeks, and now the movement was routine—tip the canoe and slide Holly against the gunwales, reach for her torso, slide her out, carry her toward the water, find a depth that was not in the main current. The rock weights were looped around my neck. With an audience it now felt like desecration to move her like that, but it was what I did. I had her body out of the canoe when all four girls came over to help lift, and I knew they didn't know what I was doing, so I had to explain. I chose the words carefully.

"I keep her submerged."

That was all I said. The girls were silent, and I sensed they were holding their breath. Holly's body secreted a smell that I'd become accustomed to, though it had to be new to them.

We walked Holly into the water until it almost crested our Muck Boots. We laid her down and held her beneath the small waves moving across the beach. I slipped off one string of weights and looped it over her upper torso. Her body moved slowly toward the lakebed. I slipped off a second string and now the other girls helped with the rocks until Holly was safely submerged and tethered. Anne and Max took my canoe up the shore and nested it with the others. Bean and Charlotte helped with my packs. I followed them inland through a stretch of marshy tundra to a high spot, flat and dry. I just then noted the absence of bugs, which hadn't swarmed me viciously since I came off the Thelon and onto the big lakes.

Anne received her callback and told me that a Mountie would fly in tomorrow morning. I stood surrounded by people and felt self-conscious. I touched my hair, now matted in places, the snarls like giant cocoons. I hadn't brushed my teeth since the accident, and I could feel the film with my tongue. I knew I stank, but I couldn't smell it. I wanted to bathe and slough off the grime of the Thelon. I walked back to the shore with Holly's P-pack and undressed. I followed a shallow beach into the lake, then lay back and submerged. It was cold, but I forced myself to stay in the water and move my hands over my body to wipe off dirt and sweat. I felt for my forehead wound, now scabbed over. It was no longer sensitive. In fact, I couldn't feel anything, the nerve endings severed. On the shore I pulled on a clean long-sleeved wool undershirt and wool leggings that were Holly's. I wore my same dirty flannel shirt that hung loosely from my shoulders and Holly's pants that I'd worn for the past few days.

Max walked up from the lakeshore dangling a cleaned trout that looked large enough to feed the five of us. They had drift-wood piled in one canoe, so they started a fire and began cooking. I was starved for real food, cooked food, and fresh protein. I told them I had plenty of pasta and rice, that half my food and the stove had been lost in a bear attack, and I rarely found wood to cook. Anne asked what I ate and I told them—mostly oatmeal, TVP, pancake and brownie mix, shortening, sugar, freeze-dried soup mix, and powdered eggs.

They unpacked an aluminum grate and I watched the trout cook over the open flames. They boiled pasta and freeze-dried veggies on their camp stove and then added orange powdered cheese sauce. Max flipped the trout and seasoned the meat with salt. When it was done, she slid the meat off the bones with a fork and set a portion onto each plate. The pot of pasta was passed, and each of us ladled out a cup scoop. I was anxious to eat, I felt starved but waited until someone took a bite, and then I started. My portion of trout disappeared in four mouthfuls. I tasted the mild fish flavor and was overwhelmed by the feel of the meat in my mouth. The skin was crispy and salty. The pasta was like the mac and cheese served in the college cafeteria, but now it tasted creamy, buttery. In minutes I was finished. I looked at my empty plate, then looked around to see the four girls just staring. Bean next to me leaned over and scraped her leftover portion of fish onto my plate. She said, "I'm just not hungry."

I said, "Thanks," and lifted a forkful into my mouth.

Anne scooped another cup of pasta onto my plate and then it was Max who came over and said, "You can have mine too."

Charlotte stood and walked toward me and I told her thanks, that I was full. She scraped her fish onto my plate. I was embarrassed but I couldn't stop eating. And then I realized that I was quietly crying, and I couldn't stop eating and I couldn't stop crying.

42

After dinner the campers laid more wood on the fire. They carried on a conversation as though I didn't exist—they had a few more days until they reached Baker Lake, and all but Anne were excited about starting college, some moving far from home. I didn't join in, which made for a bit of awkwardness, like a nervous dog new to the pack. No one looked my way and asked me what had happened on the river, how a girl close to their age had come this far and died. I thought their hesitance came from compassion, respecting a trauma I wasn't prepared to discuss. But I wanted to talk because I didn't want to keep it hidden, and I waited for a pause in their conversation. Finally, I found the words.

"She was taking a selfie and standing too close to the edge of the Thelon Canyon. She slipped and fell into the rapids. Our PLB was broken in the accident. I found your note at the cairn near the bluffs. I've been following you for five days."

They looked toward me. Anne, the counselor, was the one who spoke.

"What was her name?"

"Holly."

"Holly Stone?"

"Yes, Holly Stone. Did you know her?"

"Oh my God, Holly Stone from Kawishiwi? Yes!"

Her face turned sad. After a moment, Anne continued. "We paddled together in Manitoba on the Bloodvein River. We were close friends for that summer. The next summer we were on different trips to the Barrens, but we got together in camp when we could. I knew she was back up on the Thelon and I was hoping to see her. But not like this."

I said that I was sorry. I reached over to touch her hand and our hands lingered together for a moment. I asked her to tell me about her time with Holly on the Bloodvein.

We stayed quiet for minutes, all of us feeling the warmth of the fire and waiting. Anne was emotional. She looked up at the sky, and I could tell she was holding back tears, trying to compose herself. She shook her head slightly and then looked in my direction.

"Max and Charlotte know the Bloodvein. It begins in Ontario and then runs west and north across to Manitoba and eventually empties into Lake Winnipeg. It's almost the same landscape as here—hard gray rock covered in lichen, little topsoil, water everywhere. But on the Bloodvein there's no permafrost, and the pines, birch, and spruce grow tall. The bugs aren't as bad, and there's plenty of firewood. But you don't have the feeling there of the Barrens' total solitude. It's not the same feeling of forever, the feeling that you're the only one on the planet, a time before humans. Most of us love the Barrens for that and respect its, well, primordiality. On the Barrens you'll see the remains of a wolf or bear kill, and you'll see the bones of caribou. I've seen rock piles near the camps of Inuit, where I've picked up a stone and uncovered a human skull. You see death out on the Barrens and know that it's a part of life. I know Holly knew and felt that, and she respected that."

Max picked up a stick and poked at the diminishing fire. The campers all nodded in agreement. I also understood what Anne described.

Anne continued, "Six of us paddled for four weeks on the Bloodvein. We started at Red Lake, a small First Nations village in the middle of nowhere. Just west we hit the Bloodvein. The river can be fun—lots of class two and three rapids, easy to navigate, then some faster sets up to class six that were impassible and needed to be portaged. I paddled with Holly that trip. She liked to paddle stern, and I was okay with paddling bow. We were both experienced whitewater paddlers and ran all the rapids that we thought were class four or easier. Class five rapids are ones with a good drop, continuous whitewater, and big rocks that need precise maneuvering. You make a mistake on a class five and you're in the water. There's a rule you've probably heard. If someone in the canoe says no, then you portage or line. I was never one to say no. I think I'd do a class six if Holly didn't say no. So, it was always up to her to be the responsible one, and she said no plenty of times. For the first two weeks we shot rapids that the others portaged or lined. On two class five rapids we portaged our gear but shot the rapids just for fun, knowing there was a high likelihood of swamping. We had a counselor, but she respected our abilities and judgment, at least Holly's.

"Mid-trip we hit Artery Lake right on the border of Ontario and Manitoba. The Bloodvein widened and wandered there, not like a lake you'd imagine, not like Aberdeen or Beverly. It was an easy place to get lost. Then off the main length of the Artery ran a maze of channels, rivers almost, that went north and south, which made the Artery a crossroads for the First Nation tribes. Because the lake was a crossroads, they met there and traded. On cliff walls around the lake were pictographs. They'd been painted with a mix of hematite and fish oil, in a color like dried blood. Some were just hash marks, circles, or smears, but others were of humans and animals, and a few depicted a person in a canoe. These drawings were hundreds of years old, and there we were, paddling just as others had done over the centuries. One pictograph was of a bison with horns, others that looked like a fox or an otter. One Holly believed was called Mishipeshu, or the underwater panther. You could see the long body of a panther, a spiky horned back, a head with antlers. The Mishipeshu was supposedly one of the most powerful underworld beings, and the master of all water creatures and the water itself. The Natives had ceremonies to appease the Mishipeshu so they'd have safe passage across the lakes and rivers. Holly knew all this and told us the story as we sat in our canoes. Holly said we needed to do the same, that our ceremony would be a baptismal. She then lifted her paddle from the lake and let the water drop onto her upturned face. We all did the same. Then she said, 'Now we are safe.'"

Anne paused and looked around. I could see Charlotte and Bean smile. The thought of a ceremony to make us safe seemed real to me, connected to an undertow of natural forces. And I wondered what ceremony Holly and I had eschewed. What did we do wrong to set the forces against us?

Anne continued, "After Artery Lake, there was something like eighty sets of rapids to shoot. I was just a camper then, without the responsibility of a counselor, and I wanted to paddle every set.

Holly was the cautious one who always had to say no. I would cajole her with, 'We can do it,' and, 'Come on Holly.' I think she started to feel like the mom or the buzzkill. But I was wearing her down. Then we came to Stonehouse Rapids. Stonehouse was usually a class four chute between tight rock cliffs, a gorge really. The river was high, though, and Holly was estimating it as a class five. All six of us scouted the river, and all of us except for me agreed to portage. And on the portage with our packs, I kept hounding Holly with, 'We can do this, we got this.' She finally acquiesced. She said, 'Okay.' So, we asked our counselor, and she said, 'Fine, no packs, wear your helmets, scout your line.' And then all of us stood above the gorge and argued, then agreed on the best line. The biggest obstacle that made it a real class five was the narrow chute that dropped six feet in the course of six feet. Toward the end of the drop was a submerged rock, you could see it divert water into a rooster tail of spray. You hit that, and you're gonesville. After that drop, the rapids widened and then rolled out into corduroy lines of three-foot standing waves. The plan was to drop through the chute, keep left to avoid the rock, paddle through the next, easier set of rapids, and then slow up to hit the waves just right.

"Holly paddled stern and guided us through the entrance to the gorge. I looked up for a second, and I could see the other four in our group watching and probably cheering us on. We hit the chute perfectly, both of us calling out obstacles and strokes. At the bottom of the chute I saw the rock and quickly did a draw to get us farther left. We plowed through the rooster tail of water. Then we hit the rapids and glided through easily. Finally, the set of waves. I back-paddled to slow us up. Holly did the same and lined up our bow. Then we both paddled hard and fast down the center. I could feel us go sideways just after we hit the first wave, and I did my best to straighten out the bow, but we were going too fast. We hit the second wave at forty-five degrees and were swamped instantly by the wall of water. We both went in. I was under for like two or three minutes, caught in an undertow that held me down and crushed the air in my lungs.

"I felt a quick tug on my vest like a fish hooked on a line, and I came up gasping for air. And Holly held on to me as we both slid through the remaining waves the way we'd been trained—keeping our heads up, facing downstream with our legs and boots out front to fend off any rocks. It was over quickly, and we bobbed in the slack water below the rapids. We swam to the swamped canoe and dragged it toward the others, who were wading in to help. When it was over, when we were sitting on the shore, Holly just said, 'Mishipeshu was with us.'

"We were both good paddlers, and we'd shot plenty of standing waves in the past. It was a freak accident that we went sideways in that first wave and dumped in the second, maybe some weird twist in the flow of water—I don't know. I was caught in the wave, and Holly pulled me up. Holly saved me from almost a certain drowning. I was lucky that day. Mishipeshu was with me, but so was Holly."

We were all silent, focused on the fire dwindling down to orange embers.

Did I really know Holly? Anne had her story of who Holly was, I had my stories, Holly had her own, and she and I had the imagined stories of a life we'd never live. They all fit into a nice structure like a Freudian theory or an aboriginal myth, probably all reimagined or imagined, placating our subconscious needs at the time. There was another story.

Holly had sat down with me at the coffee shop and asked what I was doing. I said I was doing my homework, obvious, and then she asked me out. Holly that day was wearing an elaborate necklace that draped like a spiderweb across her chest. I remembered Jake's description of Ruby's handmade jewelry, *like webbing*. I wondered if this necklace was one my mother had created. I never asked and probably didn't want to know. But I thought maybe it was a sign. The rest of her outfit was all flowy, baggy hippy clothes with paisley designs. She wore round wire-rimmed sunglasses on top of her head, like something Yoko Ono would wear. Then at the art opening, she was wearing tight black leather pants, a white blouse with black stripes, and some hipster porkpie hat, wide-brimmed, almost a sombrero. And I was thinking of a few things. First, why was this very cool woman going out with me? Then how many costumes did she *have* in her closet—and to what purpose? We kissed that first date right at the party, right in front of anyone who cared, and that was thrilling. Weeks later we had sex. It turned out she had a closet full of obscure pieces she could mismatch in hundreds of different ways. Above her hanging clothes were two shelves of hats. She had a drawer full of both expensive and cheap sunglasses, and a box filled with jewelry. I never knew who she'd be when we met up for a date. And I thought she could be other things to other people. Did I know Holly? That was a big question. I *thought* I knew who she was. I could remember or maybe recreate what it felt like to be with her, and that felt consistent. I felt exhilarated and surprised. She was like a standing wave you hit broadside.

43

Early the next day the floatplane crossed over the campsite, then landed and taxied to the shore. I sat and waited and wondered what would happen next. I thought of Jake and how his paranoia of the police had rubbed off on me. My instinct was to hide, maybe lie, maybe get vengeful. Right off, I could feel Jake's thoughts channeling through me. I hugged my knees and tried to calm myself. I tried to think of something else, Anne's story, the underwater panther, and what that had meant to Holly. The idea of a water god would have appealed to her, to know that she had died on the Thelon might have been comforting—dying while doing something she loved, in a place she loved. But I knew she was far from ready for her life to end. The image of Holly standing above the canyon came to me. A stupid photo and then the fall. Finding her alive, her death, my journey downriver. The authorities would ask about all of that, and I'd have to go through it again, now in detail. I sat on the shore surrounded by the four campers as the plane's engine revved in quick bursts and pushed the two floats through the shallow water and up close to shore.

The door opened and a woman wearing a Mountie-style fur hat stepped out and onto one of the floats, then onto the beach. She was followed by a man with a blue and gold cap. The woman spoke first.

"Lee Harvey?"

I nodded. She introduced herself, Officer Yvonne Tookome, like too-coo-me, and that was what she did, speak softly, coo me, touch my shoulder. She had dark hair tied back in a knot, and the broad face, cheeks, and eyes of an Inuit. She asked me where the body was, and I looked over to Anne. Anne said she'd show the other officer, and the two walked up the shore to where Holly was weighted down under the lake. Then I went through the story of her falling from the canyon edge and dying two days later. Yvonne took notes, had me back up. How do you two know each other? Why did you want to canoe the Thelon? Where did you start? What was the name of the pilot who flew you in? What experience did you have? Did you know that the Barrens were dangerous? Where were you when Holly was taking her photo? How did Holly eventually die? How did you get the body from Thelon Canyon to Aberdeen Lake?

The details staggered from my mouth. I answered in brief sentences like I was speaking to Jake, like I'd seen him talk to a social worker or a Columbus cop, like the time they came to arrest him. I remembered then seeing Jake touch the handle of his handgun, deciding what to do, a misanthrope who said he hated society but really hated anyone who wasn't me. I was just a child, a pawn. I answered the questions but not altogether like Jake. I truly wanted her to know, and I wanted Officer Tookome, Yvonne, to understand my journey. And I knew there would be a time when I would elaborate more. I'd explain what it was like to be with Holly, where we both came from, how I came to follow her to the Thelon. I'd say what it felt like to see Holly slip, the unexpected horror of it. I'd tell how lost I was when she finally died, how alone. I'd talk about the stories I told Holly each day and night as I paddled down the Thelon. All that would come later after I understood the story better myself. Her last question, "Do you have your passport?"

"No. My clothes, my wallet, and my passport were lost. Holly was carrying my pack. I have hers."

Yvonne sat cross-legged in front of me, her notebook on her lap, scribbling away. She looked up. "You don't have *any* identification?"

"None."

Behind her I could see the other officer wade into the water and then reach down to lift the rocks. Anne waited on shore and watched. The officer pulled at the end of the sleeping bag and dragged Holly to shore. He stood there, thinking. And I could see what he was thinking, what he was going to do next—leave Yvonne with the girl, go back to the plane and get the body bag, get the pilot to help him, find something to block the view from the other campers, open the sleeping bag and unzip it from the body, photograph the decaying body, lift the body into the bag, carry the sealed bag to the plane and store it in the back fuselage, stow the packs, lash the canoe to the two struts of one float, get me in the plane. And that's what happened. All this time Yvonne was running out of questions. Finally, she took down the contact information from each camper and then led me toward the plane.

Before I left, I thanked the girls and gave each one a long hug. I hugged Anne last. She wished me good luck, then said she had something to show me. She kicked off her left Muck Boot and then lifted her pant leg. Tattooed on her calf was the long body of a panther with its spiked spine and bison antlers—the underwater panther, the Mishipeshu.

She said, "Always in memory of Holly."

44

The Mountie office looked like a cheap apartment building from the outside—wooden stairs, two storm doors, a DirectTV satellite dish. The right door opened to the RCMP office. Inside was a waiting room with folding metal chairs and a receptionist who looked at me with a sad downturned smile, like the word had already spread. Wanted posters hung from a bulletin board with community event posters, and I wondered how many fugitives had fled this far north. Yvonne's desk was in a room shared by others, and hidden somewhere was a cage for criminals. I unlocked Holly's phone and found the number for her parents under the speed-dial *Home*. Yvonne called the number and put the smartphone up to her ear.

"Is this Mrs. Stone? . . . This is Officer Tookome from the Royal Canadian Mounted Police. . . . There's been an accident. . . . I'm afraid Holly has been in an accident, and unfortunately Holly has died."

Yvonne paused and listened to whatever was taking place on the other end. I could only imagine—disbelief, crying, hysterics.

I couldn't take it anymore and I stood up. Yvonne nodded to me, and I walked from the office and took a seat in one of the steel folding chairs. The receptionist asked if I would like some coffee. I thanked her but declined, and sat there long enough to read every notice on the bulletin board, sat there until Yvonne finally came out and took the chair next to me.

She said, "Holly's parents will fly up as soon as they can, tomorrow I expect. There's the Lodge that rents rooms or the Paddle Inn. Everything is expensive in Baker Lake. Do you have a credit card or money?"

I'd never owned a credit card. The money I had with me was lost along with everything else. I said, "No."

"You can stay with me if you would like. I have a pull-out and a dog."

The offer was generous. Yvonne seemed nice, like in another world at another time we could be friends—paddle together, fish, hike, drink beer, whatever—but I didn't feel like making conversation, making friends, and I just wanted to be by myself with no questions to answer, nothing to explain. I told her she was kind but that I'd rather just be alone. I asked her if there was a place to set up my tent, and Yvonne told me about an abandoned canoe camp down the shore toward the airport. She would drive me. And since my two packs were still in the RCMP truck, I let her.

Baker Lake was orderly like a planned community, like barracks, like a trailer park. The homes looked prefabricated and were painted bright colors like robin's-egg blue, sunflower yellow, fire-engine red. It was August and sunny, and a few people walked down the gravel streets. I guessed that a town built on permafrost and iced in for most of the year had no use for pavement. The people we passed waved to Yvonne. Most were Inuit.

I looked into the driveways of homes, and that was where the orderliness ended. Caribou antlers stuck up from behind trash cans and under plank steps and against the vinyl, steel, and plywood siding. One house had a line of caribou hides draped over a rope, like laundry drying. I saw more ATVs than trucks, and more snowmobiles than ATVs. We passed a concrete wall just outside town near the lakeshore. Someone had spray-painted the graffiti, "Mary 7-18-16." Underneath that, "Mary is a whore." I didn't say anything to Yvonne.

She told me that the canoe camp was a city project to attract more tourists through Baker Lake and onto the surrounding rivers. She said that the problem was, no one told the canoers. She dropped me at one of six tent platforms set along the lakeshore next to an abandoned building the size of a two-car garage. The doors of the building were missing, and on the cinderblock exterior someone had spray-painted genitals mid-sex. I could see the graffiti artist was good, vibrant colors and detail down to the air-brushed black pubic hairs. The graffiti loomed in the background as Yvonne helped unload my packs. As a parting comment, she told me that to get back across the border I would need a new passport from the US consulate in Winnipeg. I thanked her and she drove off.

I pitched my tent on the platform. I found firewood stacked for the tourists who never came and made a fire in a ringed iron pit with a grate. I cooked rice with TVP and vegetable soup mix. I still had a craving for the fresh protein of lake trout but not as intense, not as overwhelming. I saw more graffiti, maybe written by souls surrounded by a beauty they couldn't see anymore, proximity amplified to desperation. Someone had written, "I need to get out of Baker Lake—I have no money—who do I need to blow?" Another had written, "Rhea is a whore." Underneath that, in the same handwriting but different color paint, "I'm sorry, I didn't know." Then another, "Theresa 6-28-17," and I wondered what happened to Theresa on June 28. I could see the town of Baker Lake just on the other side of an inlet. It stretched across a low hill with the brightly colored prefab houses now indistinguishable. The place reminded me of the cattle feedlot next to the packing plant just outside Columbus—all mud, cattle, fencing, and feed sheds as far as the eye could see. And I was wondering what *I* needed to do to get out of Baker Lake.

I'd never considered how Holly planned to cook the brownie mix we brought, but just then it came to me, and I stirred the powdered mix with water, powdered eggs, and melted shortening. I greased my small cook pot and added the batter. I made a double oven by putting rocks in the bottom of the larger pot and then placing the smaller one inside and covering both. I pulled the homemade oven off the fire when I smelled the mix burning. The brownies were scorched on the bottom but above that they tasted sweet and rich.

Late the next morning Yvonne drove up in the RCMP truck. The air was cold, and the sky clear and blue. I sat on the edge of the platform with the pack guitar, working on chords, trying not to think. Yvonne sat down beside me. Instead of the fur hat, she wore an official-looking blue cap with a wide gold band and crest. Her hair was tied back into an elaborate stubby braid like the tail of a show horse. We exchanged greetings, and I put down the guitar between us. She picked it up. I told her I was just learning. She played a few chords. I asked her to teach me a new chord. She gave me the guitar.

She said, "Show me what you know."

I played the four chords that I knew. She smiled.

"You have four of the five basic chords. C-A-E-D. You need G, and you have the five, C-A-G-E-D, caged. Here . . ."

She reached over and slid my three fingers to the correct strings and frets. I strummed with my right hand and I could hear the chord. I strummed again to memorize the sound and where my fingers were positioned. I counted the frets for each finger, two-one-three with three on the last string. I could remember that. I knew she was here for a reason, and now she came out with it.

"The parents are flying in. They should arrive in an hour or so. You should be there with me when they land."

I played the chord once more and nodded. I had thought maybe I would have another day to myself. I didn't think I was ready—but how could I ever be ready?

45

I knew what it was like now to lose a friend, a lover—shock, heavy grief, a question of why, an instinct to put one foot in front of the other, a longing for routine, relapses into grief, then just a deep longing. How was it for a parent to lose a child, a child like Holly? I had asked Cody once what it was like to be a guy. We were both profoundly stoned and sitting around the campfire. It was fall and cold, but no wind and the flames felt warm. I was happy. Cody thought about my question for a minute. He had this thing he did when trying to find the right thought or words, repeating, "Okay . . . okay . . . okay," filling the void of sound so no one could interrupt. He began with figuring out what we all had in common, starting with simple things, "We both shit, we both eat, we both sleep." And I helped him along, got deeper, "We both laugh, we both cry, we all dream at night, we both have aspirations or aspire to have aspirations," and he laughed at that one. "We both get sick, we all die." Then he added, "We both have sex in our own way, we all grieve, we have guilt, we have remorse, regrets, we all like music, we can both laugh and cry at the same parts of a movie, we both like to get high." Then what was different? The obvious physical stuff, and Cody went through them all. I said that most women wore clothes different from men, and Cody laughed at that because I wore Jake's clothes. Then it got down to qualifiers like *some* and *most* and *many*. "Most women cry more than men, most men are more egotistical than women. Men can be crueler than women, but women are real bitches sometimes." More laughter. Then Cody just shook his head and gave up. The conversation exhausted itself, and we decided to roll another joint. I guess what we figured out was that we all had more in common than we thought, that we were probably more ordinary than we thought. And I was thinking that Holly's parents hadn't slept, that the shock had passed, and now they were deep in grief. And as the plane descended into the barrenness of this landscape, they were trying to put one foot in front of the other. And they were trying to understand all the whys.

Like the streets of Baker Lake, the airport runway was hard-packed gravel. A terminal of sorts looked prefabricated and sat on stumpy legs above the ground. We waited in the cab of the truck and watched a small private jet land and taxi to the terminal. The jet engine powered down, and we both walked from the truck. Steps unfolded from the fuselage. I stood next to Yvonne, now self-conscious about my appearance. I was wearing a shirt that hadn't been washed in weeks—I hadn't really washed in weeks—and I was wearing pants that were Holly's, which I hoped they wouldn't notice. Minutes later the two parents descended the steps. Yvonne walked toward them, and I followed.

I could see the resemblance of Holly in her dad's face—long and narrow. He wore aviator sunglasses that shielded his eyes. His full head of gray hair was combed back from his forehead, and strands moved with the wind coming off the lake. Holly's mother walked behind him. Her sunglasses were larger, like drink coasters. The image I'd had from Holly was of her hair styled into an unnatural helmet, but she wore a lavender headwrap with only a glimpse of dark hair, a shade like Holly's. She was wearing lipstick, lips like Holly's, and I thought that applying makeup was something she did unconsciously like washing hands, that before today vanity was involved but no longer. Both were wearing jeans, and Holly's mother looked down at her black riding boots when Yvonne introduced herself, then me. The mother looked up. I tried to make eye contact through the opaque tint of her sunglasses. I didn't try to shake hands. I'd thought through my first words.

"I'm deeply sorry."

With those words, the mother covered her mouth with a hand, and she began to cry. The father moved toward her and put his arms around her shoulders. And we waited for the grief to subside, for the mother to regain her composure. Finally, she looked at me, and I could see she was puzzled. She separated from her husband.

"You're Lee?"

Holly had told her parents she was going back to the Thelon with her friend Lee. They didn't know Lee was a woman, that Holly was gay.

"Yes, I'm Lee."

A moment passed. The father stepped in then and introduced himself and his wife.

"I'm Reed, this is Martha."

I nodded my head and tried a weak smile. I said again, "I'm so sorry."

The father said, "Please tell us what happened."

Yvonne stood there. She was going to let this play out without interruption. Just me in front of Holly's two parents. I supposed it needed to play out. This would be the third time I'd explained what happened, and the hardest.

"We were a week into our trip, at the Thelon Canyon. We were portaging around the canyon. Holly wanted a picture of herself. She was standing too close to the canyon wall and slipped. She went into the rapids. There was no way to get down to her. She died two days later."

He looked at me carefully, searching every part of my face. "She was taking a photo of herself, a selfie?"

"I'm sorry, Mr. Stone."

He looked puzzled. I understood the irony or tragedy. Like a soldier who trains to go overseas, use sophisticated weapons, kill the enemy, and then dies from an infection somewhere in Kentucky. It seemed like such a waste, which it was. A question of why.

He asked, "Holly was alive for two days after the fall?"

"She was unresponsive, in a coma. She died while I slept."

He said, "I'm sure it wasn't your fault."

The comment lingered in the air, and for seconds no one spoke. I should have stayed awake and taken care of Holly. I could have revived her like I'd done at the canyon. Holly died while I rested. And I was the one who survived.

Yvonne broke the silence, "I can take you to the body."

The RCMP truck was a four-door, and the parents sat in the back. The mother was silent, and I thought I could feel her grief and tension and anger behind me. Yvonne made no small talk, no tourist guide notes on Baker Lake. Mr. Stone finally asked, "How did you get out? Did you paddle all the way to Baker Lake?"

"After the accident, I paddled for three weeks on the Thelon to Aberdeen Lake. I ran into a Native father and his son who took me to a group of girls from Camp Kawishiwi. They had a satellite phone, and I was flown out from there."

"Kawishiwi."

The exchange ended there. *Kawishiwi*. Maybe the root cause of it all, I wasn't sure. Then I heard the mother speak. There was anger in her voice. "Why did you decide to come to this godforsaken place?"

I tried to choose my words carefully. I wasn't sure if *you* meant me, or me and Holly. I chose me—it was all I could speak for. "I'd never been, and Holly asked me to come."

"What was your relationship?"

The dirt road rumbled beneath us like white noise—like a faucet running, like rapids. Yvonne drove and remained silent. She would continue to let this play out. She'd never asked me point-blank, though I was sure she assumed. And maybe she too wanted to know. And then, I thought, what was our relationship?

I'd learned to love Holly, and she took me places I'd never been. The experience changed me in ways, and I cherished every minute spent with her. Whether or not her parents wanted to hear the truth, they deserved the truth, and I wanted the honesty.

"We met at college, we were friends, and we were lovers."

The silence lasted until we turned off the road and onto the parking lot of a Tim Hortons. Next to the coffee shop was a Quonset hut with a paint-blistered sign that said BAKER LAKE FIRE HALL. Before the Stones could ask, Yvonne explained, "We have limited resources in Baker Lake. We use the walk-in cooler in the old Fire Hall for the town morgue."

The abandoned canoe camp was almost next door, maybe five hundred feet away, and I realized that camping there the night before, I was still close to Holly and adjoined to her. I left Yvonne and the Stones, telling them that I'd be at the camp. Only Yvonne looked my way, nodding with a forced smile. I started walking and didn't look back.

I sat on the edge of the tent platform and practiced the five chords. I tried the Dylan song again, "Tangled Up in Blue," trying to find each chord and work slowly through the melody. Then the image of the lyrics struck me—*a young man on the run, alone, but the past looming close behind.* I knew Holly would haunt me for the rest of my life. I thought about the word *haunt.* A ghost, an apparition, a revenant. She'd be beside me, she'd be in me, she'd appear in my dreams, she'd guide my decisions. Always. Maybe in some ways I'd *be* Holly, become Holly, and what would haunt me would be the shadow of myself that grew up in the bunker with a crazy father named Jake.

46

Holly's father walked into the canoe camp late in the morning two days later. His sunglasses were gone, and I could see his eyes, a forest green like Holly's. I started to stand, but he said not to. He sat on the platform next to me and looked out over the lake. He told me that Holly's mother was resting, using that term, *Holly's mother*, because I thought most of all that was who she was now. He looked down at the pack guitar that I'd placed between us. He must have known it was hers.

He asked, "Can you play?"

I said, "Holly was the one who played. I've tried to learn since. I just know a few chords. I'm trying."

The father touched the length of the lacquered neck. He said, "Tell me something about Holly."

Something about Holly. What I knew about her father was that he was also a Kawishiwi camper, they'd canoed together, and that Holly was closer to her father.

I said, "We met at a coffee shop. Holly just sat down and started talking. That was Holly, unafraid, spontaneous. I thought she was beautiful, and I don't know why she chose me. I was the opposite really, a loner. I grew up in Nebraska on a farm with just my father, and I'm more comfortable with chickens and goats than I am with people. I can't honestly tell you why she was attracted to me, but there she was, sitting across from me and already making plans for what we should do next. She took me to an art opening, this outrageous party. Later in the spring she took me camping over a long weekend in Vermont. We followed a trail beside a river that took us into the Green Mountains. Before that trip Holly and I spent time together, but we weren't really a couple. Over that trip, though, we became closer. And maybe because I could keep up on the trail and didn't mind camping in the woods, she asked me if I wanted to spend the summer with her in northern Canada. I told her I had no money, but that didn't matter to Holly. I guess she wanted what she wanted.

"I was very close to your daughter before we came to the Barrens, but I grew to love her as we canoed. She loved to tell stories, and one was of three men trapped in a small cabin on the Thelon through the winter months, starving. What Holly said was that proximity would either push them closer or push them farther away—amplify their relationship. The men grew closer, and so did Holly and I."

I looked up at Holly's father. I said, "I hope this doesn't make you uncomfortable."

"No," he said, "Go on."

I wanted to go on, wanted to tell him about our days on the Thelon, but I knew where that story would end. I thought about what a father would like to hear about his deceased daughter. That she loved the life she lived up until the moment she fell? That she was brave? That she was beautiful and smart? He knew these things. What he didn't need to hear was my story about transporting Holly down the river, not now. That story was about me, not Holly. I couldn't go on.

I asked him, "Weren't you a Kawishiwi camper?"

"Yes, I started at Kawishiwi when I was ten. I think a friend was going, and I talked my parents into letting me go. The camp is on Whiteside Lake near Ely and the Canadian border. The lake is remote and mostly uninhabited, and the water is spring-fed and deep. It's beautiful. I started on canoe trips but moved to mountaineering.

"My first big trip was in Wyoming, in the Big Horn mountains, the Biggies. Six of us hiked for three weeks through mountain passes, across glaciers, and past trout-filled lakes. It sounds stupid, but there's a bond that happens between campers that's unlike school or football. There's nothing to do but hike, camp, and talk. And you talk about your family and friends back home. You form bonds that last a lifetime.

"My big senior-year trip was into the Arctic National Wildlife Refuge in northern Alaska, about the same latitude as here. Holly and I had some of the same stories about the bugs and the Arctic light. Our group was on trail for eight weeks into areas just as remote as here. We didn't see anyone for the entire time we hiked. Unlike having canoes to carry our gear, we only had our backpacks, and only enough food in our packs to last four weeks, so we needed to be resupplied. A plane was supposed to make a drop along a river called the Hulahula, a funny name to say, and we'd yell it over and over that third week thinking about chocolate bars or maybe fresh meat and vegetables. *Hula-Hula*. We got to the drop site and waited, but the plane never showed. We stayed for three days, then realized we'd better keep moving.

"We started to ration our food. One ounce of pasta for dinner or one cup of cooked rice. One rye crisp cracker with a cube of cheese for lunch, and a quarter cup of trail mix for breakfast. But we did the math and knew we'd run out. Our thought was that maybe we'd run across another group of campers or maybe one of the few trappers that lived out in the backcountry. I lost thirty pounds, probably twenty pounds those last ten days after the missed drop. I was only 160 to begin with. We never ran into another soul. After those ten days we called it quits. We didn't have a sat phone, just a PLB. Our counselor, a friend for life, set off the beacon, called in the Search and Rescue guys from the Navy base in Anchorage four hundred miles away. We were evacuated the next day."

He looked at me then. "Didn't Holly have a sat phone or a PLB?"

"We had a PLB. It was clipped inside her life vest. I found it, but it had been ruined in the rapids."

I let that piece of information settle. Had that been the right place to put the PLB? Were we careless? I'd counted on Holly to know best.

The father talked haltingly, holding back tears. He said, "I wanted Holly to experience what I did. I wanted her to have those friends for life, the ones you can only bond with over weeks in the wilderness. I didn't want her to be just another city girl. And maybe that was my hubris. Maybe sending Holly to Kawishiwi was like teaching her how to ride a motorcycle or hang glide or free climb without ropes. Stupid, dangerous. You can say that life without risks is boring or unfulfilled, but I want my daughter back—desperately. I'd give my life for hers in a second."

"I don't think you could have kept Holly from taking risks."

The father shook his head. I couldn't imagine what he was thinking, and I didn't want to ask. Holly's P-pack was behind me, and I pulled it between us.

"This was hers. She fell into the rapids with *my* pack."

The pack was half full after setting up camp with the tent, her sleeping pad, and bag. He looked through it. There was a dry bag with her passport, credit cards, money, the keys to her Audi. He found Holly's folding knife. He said the knife was the same one he had on his Alaska trip. He stood with just those things. I told him that the car was parked in Winnipeg. He nodded. I told him that the guitar was also hers, and he told me to keep it, play it. He said that I should join him and his wife for dinner at six. They were staying at the Nunamiut Lodge.

47

I found a discarded plastic five-gallon bucket along the shore and filled it from the lake. I heated quarts of water in a cooking pan and mixed them back with the cold water in the bucket until the temperature was almost pleasant. In Holly's P-pack was a mini cake of soap taken from one of the hotels we'd stayed in on our way up to Yellowknife, the Airport Motor Inn just outside Winnipeg. I stripped off my Muck Boots and socks, my pants that were Holly's, and my flannel shirt. It was cold out but the bright sun felt good against my skin. My body was different now—thinner, tighter, smaller. My breasts had shrunk, nipples pointing south. A shame really. Holly loved my full breasts, and she'd want me to bulk back up, fill out. I used the quart pan to scoop water from the bucket and douse my body. I soaped up and then poured more water to rinse off. I dried off with Holly's Corona "Life's a Beach" towel. I found Holly's clean underwear and bra and a clean pair of jeans. There was also a plaid shirt of Holly's that I hadn't worn. I straightened out my tangled hair with Holly's brush. My teeth had a gritty coating that I was used to, like worn deerskin gloves, but I scrubbed them anyway with her toothbrush.

I left myself an hour to walk to the lodge but arrived thirty minutes early. I sat in an easy chair. An Inuit woman behind the desk smiled at me. She didn't say anything, and I wondered if everyone in town knew my story and who I was having dinner with. In this small town, news of a tourist death on the Thelon was probably shared, and maybe they knew some of the details from Yvonne and the other RCMP officer. Magazines lay spread out on a coffee table, old issues of *Outdoor Canada* and *Wild Guide*. I sat and waited and thought about how I should act and what I should say. The easiest thing would be to keep it simple, just the facts, like Jake—though that was not who I wanted to be anymore.

They came into the lobby and stood before me. The father, Reed, wore a dark-blue crew-neck sweater. His hair was combed tight to his scalp and looked wet. The mother's hair was tied back in a knot, her lipstick fresh. The father greeted me by name, and the mother, Martha, lifted the ends of her mouth in a tight-lipped smile. I stood and smiled and said, "Hello," then followed them into the dining room.

They sat on one side of a table for four. I was opposite and facing the lake. Martha pulled her napkin from under the knife and spoon and put it down below on her lap. I did the same. I didn't know how to start this conversation, so I just stayed silent and waited. Finally, Reed spoke. "Thank you for joining us for dinner."

"Thank you for having me."

"I appreciate your willingness to speak with us. I'm sure it must be hard for you—I know it's been hard for you. It must've been arduous bringing Holly back to us, and we appreciate that."

"Of course."

Reed paused for a moment to collect himself. "You'll have to forgive me if I say the wrong thing or ask the wrong thing. This was a great shock to us, and we haven't slept much."

"I understand."

Martha sat quietly and looked at me, and I tried to avoid meeting her stare. She let her husband move the conversation along until I realized she couldn't wait any longer.

She said, "I'm sorry, but could you please tell us what happened?"

I started to say what I'd said before to them, to Yvonne, to the campers, to the Inuit man and boy. It felt rote now, something I'd have to repeat for the rest of my life. "We were at the Thelon Canyon. She was taking a photo of herself. She slipped and fell into the rapids."

Martha stopped me. Just a small shake of her head, her mouth open and teeth clenched. "No, tell me the whole story. Tell me how you met. Tell me how you decided to take a paddling journey in this wilderness. Tell me the whole story—the beginning, middle, and end. Tell us where you came from, who you are. We have time, unfortunately, too much time now."

The father might have been closer to Holly, but it was the mother who channeled her daughter's thoughts. I remembered what Holly had said—*Start from the beginning, where you came from, the journey, what happened, and what you discovered.*

So, I started from the beginning. Like running a set of rapids, I slowed down to judge the rocks—what I should tell, what would cause needless pain. Much of the story was what I'd rehearsed on the river. I told them how Holly and I met. I told them about our camping trip. I had no plans for my summer break, and assumed

I'd stay in College Hill and work, but Holly had a vision of the two of us up on the Thelon all alone. She'd been there, one of the last remote places on earth where few others traveled. She thought she had a limited time to experience the Barrens again before outfitters brought in more tourists, or our lives took a different course, or we'd have the encumbrances of life like jobs, kids, responsibilities. Of course, I said that I would join her. Holly had the knowledge and the means, and she planned and paid for everything. I told them the story of buying the canoe. I told them how Holly would tell me stories about growing up in Saint Paul.

We ordered from a menu of three items written on a whiteboard with dry-erase markers. I think we all wanted a strong drink or a beer or a glass of wine, but the restaurant didn't serve alcohol. My pork chop and medley of carrots, onions, and broccoli tasted heavenly. We ate our dinners, and they just let me talk. I think the parents realized that if they asked questions, the story could spiral in another direction, maybe down some rabbit hole of what-ifs and could-you-haves. Their questions might shut me down, and then they'd never know. They let me talk, and I told them about the journey.

Martha cried silently while I described how we had portaged Thelon Canyon and how Holly fell into the rapids while taking a photo. How she died two days later. I'd had no way to contact the outside world and there was no going back. The river flowed toward Baker Lake, and I flowed with it. I kept Holly safe from the threats of animals and the dangers of hot days. I paddled mostly at night and kept Holly protected. I had an encounter with a grizzly and a wolverine. I found a three-day-old note from a Kawishiwi camper stuck in a cairn. I saw the smoke from their campfire once in the distance but couldn't make up the distance separating us. I was windbound for two days on Aberdeen Lake. Finally, a fishing boat passed. They took me to the campers who had a satellite phone.

I spoke through the meal and dessert and then through cups of coffee. My story, my journey, ended at Baker Lake. There was a brief silence, the two waiting for me to finish, giving me the extra time to say one more thing, but I didn't have anything more to say. I ended the story before the story was finished. I should have added something about what I discovered and how the journey changed me. But that would've been inappropriate because it wasn't about me. And what I discovered, how I changed, was something I still needed to understand myself. But I knew I'd changed.

Then Martha asked a question, anger in her voice. "I don't understand why anyone would want to go back to this desolate place."

What I didn't tell Holly's parents was the story she had for our lives. I told them now. "Holly said she wanted to have a child, a boy in her vision named Theo after the Thelon—the river meant that much to her. I also want children. If I have kids, I'll bring them here. I'll come back."

That night I stayed up late. For the first time I saw the sun disappear below the horizon and the darkness of night descend. The stars came out until the length of sky was overwhelmed with pins of light. To the north was an undulating greenish glow that seemed to emanate along the top edge of low clouds, though the sky was cloudless. Northern lights. I felt that I hadn't really seen the night sky for ages, maybe since I left Nebraska. It was an unexpected gift.

48

I couldn't fly to Saint Paul with the Stones without a passport.

Yvonne drove into my camp after they had left. I guess it was her day off because she was dressed in flannel, jeans, and Muck Boots. We could have been twins. Her hair fell in a braid that hung to the center of her back, and she wore a stupid sock monkey hat with little pink ears. She lit a cigarette and sat down on the platform. She got right to the point. She said that the Stones had left me something, and she handed across a bulging manila envelope with a string closure. I pulled out the contents—an open ticket to Winnipeg on Calm Air—the cost was twelve hundred dollars—a thick wad of Canadian currency, and a handwritten note from Reed.

Dear Lee,

We understand your situation and know that you wouldn't willingly take our help. This should get you back to the US and school. We owe you that much for what you've done and been through.

Holly was our second child, our baby girl, our special one. Martha and I tend to be too serious about life and conscious of how we appear to others. Holly showed us how to break out of our narrow paths and how inconsequential was our vanity. She also showed us how to enjoy life more, have some fun, and share stories along the way. Maybe she did the same for you, showed you what to value in life.

Of course, we valued and loved Holly and will miss her greatly. I'm sure you share that loss. I'm sure she'll live inside us all forever.

There will be a service in St. Paul at St. John's Episcopal Church. We welcome you there but understand if you find it difficult. Regardless, you are always welcome at our home, consider yourself part of the family.

Sincerely,
Reed Stone

It was what I also felt, that Holly showed me how to look at life around me differently, that experience was the fabric of life, and that nothing was preordained by the past. That she'd live inside me forever. Yvonne put her arm around my shoulders then, and it felt good to be held and touched.

I gave her the food pack, still half-full of supplies, to use herself or donate. I told her she could have the bandaged red canoe, the fifteen-foot Royalex Mad River Quest with no seats. I told her the story that had been told to Holly and me, about the original owner, Jack London, and his trips through the Barrens and his ultimate demise on the Muskox Rapids of the Coppermine River. I told her that I thought the canoe was bad luck and ill-fated, and that it might be better used upside down on a stack of cut fire-wood to keep it dry. Yvonne smiled and lit another cigarette. She told me that the plane to Winnipeg left daily at 9 a.m. She gave me a last hug, and we said our goodbyes.

I took Holly's P-pack with my few clothes mixed with hers. I also traveled with the tent and sleeping bag. In Winnipeg I rented a room at the Airport Motor Inn, the same place where Holly and I had stayed weeks before, while waiting for a flight to Yellow-knife. The circle was complete.

I left Winnipeg days later with an emergency passport that would get me across the border. The bus traveled overnight and arrived in Saint Paul the next morning.

I owed it to Holly and her parents to be at the funeral. I found the church in a neighborhood of Victorian-era buildings, a short walk from the bus station. I imagined Holly growing up in one of the old mansions that lined Summit Avenue—her own room, Christmases with a huge tree and lots of presents, close friends in the neighborhood who would be at the funeral. I learned the time and date of the service, which was the next day.

I found a cheap motel near the Mississippi River and walked in the woods at the water's edge. The elm trees along the banks had trunks the width of full-grown musk ox. The Mississippi was nothing like the shallow, muddy Platte, or the clear Thelon that snaked through the expanse of the Barrens. It moved swiftly in a deep and wide channel large enough for commercial barges. Just sitting by the moving water felt soothing—the water con-necting me to home and to Holly.

I arrived at the church minutes after the service had started. I sat in the back and listened as Holly was eulogized. Every-one knew Holly in their own way. The priest remembered Holly as a child taking communion, before Holly stopped going to church. A teacher remembered a girl with a thirst for knowledge who would read two books for every one assigned, a precocious student who questioned everything, who made her teachers question everything. A neighborhood boy, a close friend, told a story about winter camping and building an igloo. The igloo collapsed in the middle of the night. People laughed. He knew her as someone who was fearless. An aunt spoke for the family and talked about the cabin on a lake near the Canadian border. She spoke about the times around the campfire when Holly, full of life, would play her guitar and lead the songs. I sat in the back with my own memories and stories of the Holly I knew.

I wrote a card to the family that I set with the others. I was the first to leave the church—I just couldn't meet people and tell the story of our trip on the Barrens. The note in the envelope was something I'd said to myself over and over as I paddled the Thelon, "I miss her so much."

49

After getting off the Thelon and back to College Hill, I sent Jake and my teacher, Lonnie, a long email that described what happened. The message had taken me a week to write and edit, and even then, I felt I hadn't really said what I wanted. But I'd given myself a week, and at the end of that week, the night before classes started, I read through the story. I thought I'd described as well as I could how the Barrens appeared and how they felt to me. I talked about our canoe, Quest, and who Holly was and what she meant to me. I described what happened at Thelon Canyon and the aftermath on the river. When I first wrote the description of the accident, I had a nightmare, the same vision of falling with Holly, the rocks approaching as we plummeted. The next morning, I forced myself to write about the nightmare and then forced myself to rewrite the description of the accident. I guess my idea was to exorcise the trauma of that memory. The nightmare didn't recur, but I wasn't sure it wouldn't haunt me forever. So that last night I reread the email. I realized it wasn't all there. I'd missed so much—how Holly had changed me, who I was now. I gave myself until midnight but realized I wasn't entirely sure myself. I spent the last hours adding words, adding a few descriptions, reluctantly deleting whole paragraphs. I pressed *send*.

Back at Brown I felt different, untethered with a wide range of choices, and Nebraska felt so far away. One of the choices I made was to study literature in addition to mathematics. I'd enrolled in a freshman English course and talked my way into a creative writing class. The writing professor was a young woman who'd written mostly short stories about people in northern Minnesota. I read one collection that included a piece about canoeing in the Boundary Waters. What resonated were her descriptions of being on the water. In one, she described paddling in the early morning before the sun emerged above the horizon, the gloaming. She described the sound of the paddle dipping into still water. It made me cry. Eventually, I wanted to write about those same things but in my own way, in my own voice. For now, I was sticking with stories about living off the grid in Nebraska.

The students took turns workshopping their stories. The nervousness of submitting my first short story kept me from sleeping the night before, and on the day, I was tempted to skip class altogether. But I didn't. Each student critiqued my work while I kept silent with my head down writing notes. Some were gentle, some flattering, and some were outright belittling. The professor spoke last. She was always kind and supportive. I thought she knew that we were putting ourselves on the line creatively and emotionally, that we were fragile. She said what most lacked in a young author's stories was simply life experience—they hadn't lived through *unique* experience. Unique was hard to find, it transcended the everyday and brought us to an unexpected place with unexpected emotions. She said she thought my writing was unique. Her words gave me the encouragement I needed to keep writing, to honor Holly and keep telling stories.

50

I received an email from Martha, who said she'd be in Providence the next weekend to clean out Holly's apartment. She'd be alone and asked if I could help. I responded and let her know that I would.

It was the second week in October, and the leaves were just starting to turn. The sun was out, and it was one of those days where the students could be down near the river playing touch football or reading on a blanket or walking hand in hand. I was out there too, dressed in my old jeans that bunched around the waist and a sweatshirt that hung from my shoulders. My clothes reminded me of who I was, my bulk an armor against what others expected. I walked along the Providence River and crossed over on the College Street Bridge. Below I saw the water spill to each side of a piling, forming a wake and a corduroy line of standing waves. I stood for a moment with those sounds. Past the bridge, I walked down Westminster to the Goodwill. I found a pair of jeans that fit me and a dark blue V-neck sweater that made me look sexy, and just that thought, *sexy*, was new for me, surprising like the first tenderness of budding breasts.

Farther down Westminster was another used clothing shop, more vintage wear for those trying to be alt-glamorous or shabby-chic or cheap-chic or whatever. I found a thick, dark blue wool coat, like a peacoat but longer with military-looking silver buttons. I tried it on, and now I thought I looked more cool than sexy, almost chic-chic. It made me think of Holly and her costumes. It cost one hundred dollars. Then I saw this hat, brown felt with a wide brim and a narrow Indian-beaded band. It fit, and I looked good with my long hair held in place and covering my ears and shoulders. The hat was fifty bucks. Then I tried on the military wool coat with the hat. I could see that the brown and the blue contrasted or clashed, but I liked the look. The crown was pinched and creased like a cowboy hat, maybe a cowboy hat a Plains Indian would wear. Last semester I'd watched *Dances with Wolves* with Holly at her apartment, and I was thinking that this was my post–Civil War, Western Plains look—my costume. Maybe fitting for a girl from Nebraska. One hundred and fifty bucks for the two items seemed extravagant, but I bought both. Holly would have approved. I crossed back over the bridge holding two large bags full of new used clothing. I thought that I might return to the same Goodwill next week with the bags filled with my old clothes that no longer fit—Jake's clothes.

I SAT ON the steps of Holly's apartment building early on Saturday morning when Martha arrived in a Lincoln Town Car. Her helmet of hair was brushed back from her forehead, volumized, and held in place by spray. She wore sunglasses and a mink coat—the mink Holly said her mother had only worn indoors. The trunk of the car popped, and Martha asked me to help her carry in the few empty boxes. Her greeting was soft, almost apologetic. Disarming.

"Lee, so nice to see you."

The whole hugging culture never quite caught on in Columbus, and I wondered, *Do I hug her, put out my hand, or just go for the boxes?* We'd never hugged in Baker Lake, we never even touched. I went for the boxes. Martha had a key and let us in. She asked how I'd been, how school was going. I enjoyed college, and the routine kept me focused. I wasn't going to fall apart; I'd move forward with my life and honor Holly with my choices. What I told her was that school was going fine. On the sixth floor, Martha let us into the apartment. Nothing had changed. I asked her to let me know how I could help. She told me that she just came for a few personal items, that a service would come by to pack and deliver whatever remained to a charity.

She surveyed the room. On the TV stand was a family photo. She held it up, smiled, and stood it on the dining table. I assumed the dining table was where Martha would place the things she wished to ship home. I sat on my knees with a roll of tape. She spoke from behind me.

"Do you want the TV, the stereo?"

I had Holly's pack guitar that I was starting to get better on. I'd been watching YouTube videos and practicing more chords. I knew a half dozen songs now. I was learning "Galileo." I still had a few of her clothes from the Thelon, and I didn't really want any more of her stuff. Somehow it didn't seem right, and I thought Holly's mother, Martha, would be disappointed if I did—maybe the greediness of it.

"Thanks, no. I have a small dorm room that I share with another student. I barely have room for my laptop."

Martha was in front of me, now sitting on a dining room chair. I looked up to her as she spoke. "We were able to get into Holly's iTunes account. We were able to download her photos. They go back to her sophomore year in high school. Some photos were recognizable to me—her friends, classmates, teachers. We did ski trips to Colorado and spring trips to the Caribbean. There were photos of the family and selfie photos of herself, like the funny faces you'd make in the mirror, or at least that's what I did as a child. Then there were photos completely unrecognizable. She had friends I never knew about, a life I never understood. I saw photos of you that I could send along.

"Maybe you know this already from Reed, but I thought that when Holly said she was going back to the Thelon with someone named Lee, I assumed you were male. I was pleased to think that Holly had a boyfriend. In high school she hung out with a group of both male and female friends. They called themselves the Outsiders, like the eighties movie. But I guess I should've known better. Two of the boys dated and went to prom together. Holly and the rest of the Outsiders went to prom as a group. She did go out on dates with boys, but nothing was ever serious. Now that I've seen her photos, I know more. And maybe I knew then but didn't want to know. I had this vision of Holly going to college, finding someone, and getting married. I had this fantasy of two families getting together at our club and witnessing a marriage between two beautiful people. I can still picture the dress. Then there was the fantasy of grandchildren—beautiful, smart children who'd show up at our cabin, on vacations, and at Christmas. I could see Holly teaching her kids how to canoe. She'd send them to Kawishiwi."

I felt uncomfortable listening to her expectations about Holly's heterosexual life. They were something I knew of but hearing them stung, and I couldn't let the sentiments go completely unchecked. I said, "Holly talked about the two of us having kids."

"You said she wanted children."

"She imagined us getting married, just not at the country club. She wanted a family, one child. She wanted to carry the baby."

"All I ever wanted was for Holly to be happy. Nothing else really mattered. It doesn't matter now, and I'm happy for Holly that she found someone to love."

Martha held the photo of her family. I looked up to see the corners of her mouth quivering and tears forming at the edges of her eyes. I stood then and sat in the chair next to her. I touched her hand. Martha placed the photo back on the table. Her fingers reached for mine.

She said, "This is really hard. I'm glad that you're here with me."

"It is really hard."

"We need to keep moving."

I stood then and walked around the counter and into the kitchen. I told Martha that I'd make coffee. I waited there while she moved into the bedroom. I heard drawers opening and closing. I heard her go through the closet. Then silence. I knew that one of the photos from the art exhibit was leaning on the wall in the closet. It was a torso photo of Holly naked. Martha walked into the living room holding the photo. She looked at me and looked at the photo. She smiled. "This will be yours."

"Okay."

Martha leaned the photo against the wall next to the front door. The image faced the wall.

"Lee, I know nothing about you. Tell me something. Tell me who you are."

"I'm from a small town, Columbus, Nebraska."

"I know Columbus. You wouldn't guess it, but I grew up in a small town not far from there, David City. My father was the town attorney. Reed and I met in college. I married into the Stone family. But I'm sorry, I want you to tell me your story. Please go on."

And I did. I poured both of us coffee. I stood behind the kitchen counter and talked as Martha moved through the apartment. I'd thought about my story—Holly had made me think about my story, and it was something I was trying to describe in my writing. It was the story of a child growing up without a mother and with a father who lived by a set of unattainable ideals as best he could, a father who could be devoted but also demanding, steadfast, paranoid, selfish, and hypocritical. He brought his daughter into his idealistic world that began to crumble at the edges. And it was her existence that ate at the edges and finally shattered his life. The story had a set of details—the bunker, the river, the woods, the town, the school, Lonnie, Cody, weed, college, jail, and prison. The story of Jake was tragic up to this point, but maybe unfinished.

Martha was listening as I talked, and she told me to keep talking as she went back into the bedroom. She came out just as I finished my story.

"So, your father is still in the penitentiary?"

"For at least another five years."

"Then we can expect you for Christmas? I'll arrange it."

Her invitation was surprising and caught me off guard. I had Lonnie back in Nebraska who I wanted to see, but maybe not until next summer, and I'd visit Jake. I had a grandfather I planned to finally meet for Easter, and Christmas was something I'd always wanted to experience. It felt like I had people who wanted to be with me. And I wanted to be with them—no more bunkers, no more alone games. I was finding *my* people.

I said, "I think that would be nice."

By the afternoon Martha had only filled one box. I carried it down to the waiting Town Car and lifted it into the trunk. I stood there with my arms stiff at my side, wondering how I should say goodbye. The decision was settled when Martha approached me quickly and wrapped her arms around my shoulders. My arms lifted to embrace her in return, and we hugged in that stillness. Moments later she unwrapped her arms and stepped past the driver holding the car door. She waved from inside. A smile that said we'd just begun.

51

The first snow hit on a Friday the second week of November. My headaches still forecasted an impending storm, but by morning the pain in my sinuses had cleared. I rowed on the school's club team, and by seven thirty I was out on the Providence River, second seat on an eight-woman rowing shell. The snow falling on the water was beautiful and reminded me of crossing Aberdeen Lake in August. I'd learned that the river and rowing were calming, meditative, and the exercise set my mind right for the rest of the day. It seemed funny, ironic, that after my emancipation from Jake, I'd taken up his same college sport. And like Jake, I was good at it.

After practice I walked to a neighborhood coffee shop, the Crema, to get some homework done. I was wearing my Muck Boots, wool military coat, and the felt cowboy hat. In a shop window I could see my reflection. A light coating of snow dusted the hat's floppy brim and my face was obscured in shadow. I hardly recognized this girl. It was me, and it wasn't me. I shook off the snow-dusted hat and stepped closer to the window. The scar was there, the fat pink leech just above my left brow. Sometimes I touched it unintentionally like some students twirl a pencil or snap gum. I felt it now. At first the severed nerves had kept the wound numb, but then one side regained feeling, sensitive like the touch of a feather.

Inside the café I gave my hat a good shake then found an open table to unload my gear. I ordered a large coffee and stirred in cream and two teaspoons of sugar. The taste was like coffee candy. I sat down, opened my laptop, and pulled out a book along with my class notes. The café was full of other students doing the same, mostly women.

At a table near the window was another student I'd seen around campus. She was in front of an open laptop and typing. She wore wool tights tucked into Frye boots with square toes. Her hair was long, thick, and brown. She then reached across her face and pulled her hair up and over to hang away from her eyes, and she tilted her head to keep the hair to that one side. The movement of the hand and hair and head was attractive to me, unconsciously I guess, because I couldn't explain *why* it was attractive. Now I couldn't focus on my work. I had a distant longing not to be alone. I wanted the closeness of touch.

I thought of Holly on that first day we met, a different coffee shop but familiar with the same sounds and smells. I remembered seeing her stand up with a cup of coffee and walk to my table. She sat in the empty chair across from me. I looked up, startled.

"Yes?"

"What are you doing?"

"Homework."

I smiled behind a feigned looked of annoyance. I was wearing a flannel shirt under a wool sweater, two sizes too large. I closed the screen of my laptop and waited through an uncomfortable silence. Holly took a sip of coffee and put the cup on the table. She gave me her best smile, one that said, *Come on—we both know.*

Acknowledgments

This novel would never have seen the light of day without the belief and passion of our agent, Philip Turner, who went beyond the call of duty by soliciting author blurbs when there wasn't a publishing deal to be had, then sticking to it until there was. Then thanks to our editor, Cal Barksdale, for his belief in the novel and for his hard work in making *The Barrens* a polished work of art and thanks to our enthusiastic publicist, Kim from L.A., for her work in finding a wider audience.

A special thanks to the esteemed writer Peter Geye, whose yearlong novel-writing course was the catalyst that set this novel in motion. Peter read a first draft and provided critical edits.

There were many who helped along the way. First readers include sister and aunt, Kristi Leer; mother and grandmother, Dolores Johnson; friends Tricia Schulte, Lori Barghini, and Sarah Collins; and of course, wife and mother, Stephanie Hansen, whose never-ending support kept spirits and momentum high. Also, thanks to members of the Stone Arch Writers'

Workshop who've been helpful and supportive as we've all pursued our writing dreams.

Ellie specifically wants to thank the staff and campers at Camp Widjiwagan for providing young kids the opportunity to experience the outdoors in a way that's more than just camping but a total immersion into nature. Also, thanks to her trail mates on her journey through the Barren Lands of Canada: Kate Blankinship, Lucy Soderstrom, and Maura Wheelan. Friends forever!